COMEDY GIRL

ELLEN SCHREIBER

KATHERINE TEGEN BOOKS
An Imprint of HarperCollins*Publishers*

Library of Congress Cataloging-in-Publication Data
Schreiber, Ellen.
Comedy girl / Ellen Schreiber.— 1st ed.
p. cm.
Summary: Shy, seventeen-year-old Trixie Shapiro, who dreams of
being a professional comic, gets a big break after her friend signs her
up to do a stand-up routine at their school's Talent Night.
ISBN 0-06-009338-2 — ISBN 0-06-009339-0 (lib. bdg.)
[1. Comedians—Fiction. 2. Bashfulness—Fiction. 3. Self-realization—
Fiction. 4. Interpersonal relations—Fiction.] I. Title.
PZ7.S3787Co 2004   2003025280
[Fic]—dc22   CIP
                                                          AC
Typography by Hilary Zarycky
1 2 3 4 5 6 7 8 9 10

First Edition

To my grandpa, Aaron Schreiber,
who always made me laugh, and to my uncle,
Barry Schreiber, for having a sense of humor
when we needed it most.

Comedy Is Not Pretty!
—STEVE MARTIN

CONTENTS

OPENING

FEATURING

HEADLINING

OPENING

★ ★ ★

HEEEERE'S . . . TRIXIE!

☆

"I loathe high school. I'm unbearably shy—afraid to speak up in class. I'm not the class clown—I'm the class mime!"

I smiled from ear to ear as the audience burst into laughter. I felt an enormous rush from the packed house. Though I was onstage alone, I found comfort in my best friends: a cordless microphone, a stool, and a glass of water.

Anything could happen in comedy. The audience might not laugh, they might heckle me, they might walk out. But despite those grim possibilites, I felt unbelievably euphoric and alive.

"It's great to be here in Chicago—at Chaplin's, where I got my start. I go to a totally huge high school in the suburbs. It's so big, by the time I get to History class a new president is in office!"

I smiled as they laughed again. "My best friend, Jazzy, is a shopaholic. Always ready for the latest bargain. I walk through the school lunch line with a tray. She walks through with a grocery cart." After the laughter subsided, I continued: "She's the only student at Mason High who buys lunch with a credit card."

I took a sip of water and replaced the glass on the stool.

"I call my mom Sergeant because it's nicer than calling her Dictator. She keeps tabs on me wherever I go, like I was one of her third-grade students. While I was on the road doing comedy, she won the gold medal in the Olympics. She took first place in Women's Long Distance Calling!"

I kept my pace going. "My dad hasn't moved from the couch for years. While other fathers collect stamps, my father collects dust.

"I also have a drugged-out older brother, Sid. We used to wrestle and box when we were little. Now the only hits he takes are from a bong.

"As for my love life, I'm hoping to marry my major crush—Gavin Baldwin. I have something borrowed and something blue. I just need one more thing—the groom!"

The audience laughed again. I felt an electric connection. I was in the one place in the world where I belonged.

"The weather in Chicago—," I continued.

"Trixie, it's time for supper!" my mother called.

I looked at my seventeen-year-old reflection, then

reluctantly turned away from the mirror and my audience of adoring, wide-eyed stuffed animals lined in rows on my dresser. I switched off my tape-recorded laugh track, threw my round hairbrush microphone down on my white fluffy bedspread, and stepped out of my bedroom—back into reality.

REALITY

☆

R eality was an ordinary lavender bedroom in an ordinary redbrick home at 1414 Chandler Street in
tree-lined Amber Hills, an ordinary suburb in
north Chicago. But on occasion it magically turned into
a Beverly Hills mansion with a glistening star-shaped
pool, home to the hottest celebrity parties—all through
the technology of my vivid imagination. I invited Robin
Williams, Bill Cosby, Billy Crystal, Garry Shandling,
Roseanne, and a thousand other actors and comedians.
One night I would be accepting a Commie from Ben
Stiller for my starring performance in *"T" Is for Trixie*;
another night I would be interviewing Whoopi Goldberg
on the *Trixie Shapiro Show*.

Outside my bedroom I didn't fit in. I wasn't a cheerleader; I wasn't a nerd. I wasn't a Prudy Judy, or a druggie girl. I wasn't a loner, or a Ski Club member. I had no
label to cling to. I was just Trixie Shapiro—a girl trying
to find her place in the world.

I had grown up on Monty Python and had gotten high

on Richard Lewis. While my older brother experimented with pot, I experimented with impressions. Sid's bookshelves were lined with Stephen King, mine with Ellen, Lily Tomlin, Rita Rudner, Jon Stewart, and Jelly Bean. Sid blasted Smashing Pumpkins, Red Hot Chili Peppers, and Bush on his supercolossal, gazillion CD changer, while I quietly listened to Redd Foxx, Lenny Bruce, and Richard Pryor on Sarge's old stereo. Sid's bedroom walls were covered with posters of malnourished supermodels, while my walls were graced with the portraits of talented comediennes.

One night I was performing stand-up on the *Douglas Douglas Show*, the next headlining a Showtime special, and the next collecting my prize money for Outstanding Comic on *Celebrity Search*. Though I was small, I had large dreams. And like many of the comedians I idolized, I was painfully shy. My stage was my bedroom. My only audience was a bunch of stuffed animals.

Just as a girl remembers her first kiss or a boy remembers his first home run, I remember my first laugh.

Before I began performing alone in front of my mirror, Sid decided I should perform vaudeville acts with him in our living room for my first paying house—Sergeant, Dad, and Aunt Sylvia. For fifty cents a head they watched as I, complete with fake arrow through my head, cowered behind Sid while he performed silly skits in a blond wig and lady's sunglasses.

He and I had spent hours making programs out of construction paper for our debut performance. We pasted our elementary-school photos above hand-printed bios. Sid had starred in the Broadway production of *Scooby-Doo*, while I had just completed *Curious George Goes to the Catskills*.

One time, after our tireless rendition of "Old MacDonald," Sid struggled with his costumes behind our black leather couch—our official changing area.

"Get out there, shrimp!" he ordered me. And with a shove he pushed me out from behind the safety of the couch.

I stood alone in the middle of the living room.

Now I was the center of attention—not my older doofus brother. I, alone, was expected to entertain the audience. All eyes were on me. I stared back at my family. I was embarrassed, anxious, self-conscious. Too frightened to run, speak, or faint.

The fear of what to do, what to say, was compounded by my familiarity with my audience. What if I disappointed them?

"Say something, stupid!" Sid commanded from behind the sofa as he hurried to change into his cape. "Tell a joke!"

I only knew one joke, a silly child's joke I had created that morning in the bathtub.

My mouth was dry. I took a deep breath.

"What is Bullwinkle's favorite ice-cream flavor?" I mumbled.

"I dunno!" they answered in unison. "What is Bullwinkle's favorite ice-cream flavor?"

"Chocolate and vanilla squirrel!" I shouted.

It was my very first punch line.

And then it happened. My family laughed a huge laugh—I even heard Sid cackling from behind the couch. The laugh hit me like a bolt of lightning.

For that moment I wasn't Sid's pesky little sister, a messy kid spilling Kool-Aid on Mom's clean floor, or a daughter whining as her dad desperately tried to watch ESPN.

That laugh was like a huge hug. It was life wrapping its arms around me and squeezing me.

Then it ended. Sid jumped over the couch in a magician's cape, reclaiming the spotlight. I was immediately thrust back into my little sister role, assisting the Amazing Sidney—by disappearing!

I dreamed of reaching my comedy high again. But I couldn't push myself out from behind the couch. It would be years before I would be taking center stage again.

I went back to cowering behind Sid, but I never forgot the rush I felt from that first laugh.

Sid and I grew up not with a single imaginary friend, but many. We had a whole imaginary school system—some had to be bussed in from other parts of Illinois!

Eventually Sid began playing football with unimaginary boys and I made real, unimaginative friends.

Since I was the smallest Shapiro at home and the shortest kid in my classes, I used humor to get myself out of awkward situations. For example, class picture day in the second grade, I was afraid of sticking out in the front row. So naturally I was cowering in the back row with my taller friends.

"Girl with the reddish hair," the photographer said, staring straight at me. "Will you please stand up?"

"But I am standing!" I joked.

The whole class laughed, including the photographer. I even got a high five from the best kickball player in class.

I felt a surge of euphoria. I had to leave the company of my taller friends and march around the entire class to the first-row chairs. Instead of being embarrassed about my lack of height, I felt empowered by my sudden acceptance. Now I was the one in control and the center of attention. And I liked it.

I had a huge desire to be famous. To be best friends with the Glam Girls and recognized and adored by the hunky boys. As I continued through elementary and middle schools, I envied the popular, more outgoing girls. I wondered how, at eleven, some girls were developing breasts while I was developing material.

But all I could do was continue to write, perform my act in my bedroom, and dream.

Sarge spent forty hours a week bossing third-graders around at Harrison Primary School and then spent the rest of the time bossing her family around. Even in my dreams, the woman was straightening my room!

Dad was an accountant. When he wasn't crunching numbers he was munching peanuts in front of the TV.

Sid rebelled against the Shapiro Establishment by secluding himself in his black-lit bedroom with twelve kinds of incense seeping through the keyhole. Finally he went off to college, leaving me to face high school from behind the couch—alone.

At Mason High freshmen were thrown into the bushes behind the baseball field, were made to act as servants and carry seniors' textbooks, and force-fed Spam in the cafeteria. But hazing was also a road to friendship, and I made a best friend when Jazzy and I were literally thrown together by a gang of upperclassmen.

"Did you get any thorns?" a tall bleached-blond girl asked with concern. She offered me her hand, as I struggled to escape the prickly bush that had snagged my sweater. I stumbled out with her generous help.

"No . . . not this time," I said, pulling pricklies out of my sweater. She ignored the twigs entangled in her own hair.

"I thought they only did this once to freshmen, like an initiation," she said.

"Are you kidding? I have my own special bush. It's smaller than the others."

Her concern turned to a smile and she laughed.

"But it's okay. I rent it out on the weekends to the preschool," I teased.

She laughed again. "You crack me up. My name's Jazlyn, but 'bush girls' call me Jazzy."

"My name's Trixie. I don't like to use the name people call me."

"And what do people call you?"

"Shrimp."

"You're a hoot," she replied, towering over me. She put her arm on my shoulder and looked up at the looming high school. "Let's stick together. With my height and your attitude—you may be tiny now, but some day, girl, you'll be huge! And I don't mean dress size!"

The popular kids at Mason were the ultrarich—those who lived in mansions with two staircases and drove their parents' BMWs. I lived in a redbrick home in Amber Hills with only one staircase, and I took public transportation. Needless to say, it wasn't good enough to get me into popular parties.

In grade school I hid behind Sid. Now in high school I hid behind Jazzy. We both shared the same middle-class status, but differed in our personalities. Jazzy knew all the teachers on a first-name basis. The teachers didn't even know I was enrolled! Jazzy was model tall and I was kindergarten small. She was a bottle blonde, while my hair looked like an orange peel. But we were inseparable. When we weren't gazing at boys, we were telling jokes in our bedrooms and giggling until our stomachs felt like they would explode.

It was autumn, senior year, and Jazzy and I met for study hall in the auditorium. The auditorium was preferable to the cafeteria, which always smelled of burned hamburger. But the auditorium had its own distractions. The naked stage stole my attention. The faded red curtains looked like they had been hanging since the days of Shakespeare. The unvarnished wooden stage appeared huge, empty, and lonely, coming to life only when off-key teenagers pranced around its loosened boards.

"Talent Night is next week," Jazzy whispered, following my gaze. "We'll be up there soon."

I hated the thought of Mr. Janson's Senior Talent Night. It was our biggest assignment in Drama class, our final exam for the first quarter: prepare a solo piece to be performed in front of the entire school. No mirrors, no stuffed animals—not even Sid to hide behind.

"Are you nervous?" Jazzy asked.

The thought of actually standing on that stage and reciting Tennessee Williams or singing "Memory" shot bullets of fear throughout my body. "Unfortunately I won't be able to make it because I've joined the Peace Corps. I'll be digging wells in South America!"

"I'm going to tap-dance to Madonna's 'Like a Virgin,'" said Jazzy.

"I don't think that's a tap number."

"That's why it'll be funny. Okay, I know it's stupid! I know I'm not a comedian," she said, and buried her head in her algebra book.

My eyes remained glued to the empty stage, wishing I was one.

The spotlight was shining down on me, the heat from its powerful rays warming my body. Everyone was applauding—

14

Sergeant, Dad, Sid, my classmates and teachers. Gavin was
standing in the front row. As I took a final bow, he tossed me
a bouquet of roses.

"Look, your leading man has arrived!" Jazzy said,
nudging me with a sharp elbow.

If I could go out with one guy in the whole school, in
the whole world, it would be Gavin Baldwin. He's made
my heart throb out of my chest for years. His wild jet-
black hair begs to be touched. He has dreamy deep baby-
blue eyes and a smile that ignites fire in my soul. He
wears a gold thumb ring and dresses in traditional hipster
black. Coolness oozes from his skin.

At 10:55 A.M. Monday, Wednesday, and Friday, he
slithered in sexiness as he walked to American History
class. My favorite time of the day, the time when I
could pass his groovy self in the corridor on my way to
Algebra 2. And if I was lucky, I could gently brush up
against him.

The wonderful thing about Gavin, and why I loved
him more than a front-row seat to Chris Rock, was that
he did something the other coolheads didn't do when
they glanced in my direction—he smiled. This miracle
had happened seven times. The first time occurred when
he was parking his blue Volvo and Jazzy pulled in next to
him. He smiled at me three times when we passed in the

hallway at 10:55, twice as we waited in line for turkey and gravy in the cafeteria, and once when I was on my way to the bathroom and he was waiting for the water fountain. Gavin's deep blue, dreamy eyes pierced straight through me and his soft lips glowed like a marquee that read: KISS ME! For those seven moments we connected.

But today Gavin walked by me without making eye contact. Suddenly a female skeleton with hair caught up with him and the giggling couple plopped down in the fifth row. Gavin snuggled close to his anorexic super-model girlfriend—his tragic flaw. Spiral binders and a hard wooden armrest were the only barriers between them.

"If he only knew his true love was over here, sitting next to me," Jazzy said supportively, "he'd give Stinkface Travers das boot!"

"I can't compete with her. She's magazine glam and spends all her time getting waxed! She was left back in kindergarten, which means she has an extra year's growth in the boob department."

"Get out!" Jazzy laughed.

"She's so big," I teased, "her bra should be on display at Ripley's Believe It or Not Museum!"

Jazzy laughed again. "No, she's just got a daddy who's a plastic surgeon," she comforted me.

"Her body's so perfect, she got an A in Anatomy—

without taking the class," I continued, on a roll.

Jazzy and I giggled. "Quiet down over there," Mr. Barker scolded.

I wouldn't have been able to survive this kind of trauma without a true-blue friend like Jazlyn Peters.

LOVE AND LAUGHTER

Before that first smile from Gavin in the school parking lot, I'd had a comical series of "drive-thru" relationships with the opposite sex. The first was Mickey Collins in preschool. I, the patient, was lying on my back on the floor in my red Healthtex dress, and Mickey, the doctor, was kneeling over me with a long wooden spoon. Fortunately Miss Burke discovered us before any diagnosis was made.

Later I had crushes on numerous elementary-school dreamboats. In fifth grade I liked Nicholas, a neighborhood boy who attended a private grammar school. I received my first kiss while playing hide-and-seek one night before dinner. Unfortunately I was too skilled at the game, and when he finally did hunt me down he was exhausted. He missed my mouth and wound up kissing me on my cheek, panting more from exhaustion than love, and was then called in for dinner. I learned to leave a leg showing!

Junior year I had just experienced smile number one

from new transfer dreamboat Gavin Baldwin, when I encountered erotic oddball Eddie Abels.

It was a rainy Friday night. My parents were at a party and had left me an envelope with forty dollars "for dinner and emergencies," along with a stack of coupons for every restaurant in Amber Hills. Jazzy was spending the night, and our stomachs were growling like bears by the time the doorbell finally rang. The delivery guy from Pizza Town looked strangely familiar.

"It's Eddie from my Geometry class!" I feverishly whispered to Jazzy in the foyer, as we hung back in our nightshirts. He sat in the first row and I in the last, both daydreaming about life outside the lines of isosceles triangles. We hardly knew each other existed.

Eddie shuffled awkwardly in his red-and-blue polo shirt and bright red pants. His wet blond hair dripped out from beneath his Pizza Town cap.

"Hey, babies," he said, leaning against the doorway, eyeing my exposed legs with his sexy eyes, like he had been delivering pizzas and passion all his life.

"One large Sicilian with everything," he said, unzipping the red warming box.

I nudged Jazzy and whispered, "Without cheese."

"I hope there's no cheese on it," Jazzy interjected. "She's lactose intolerant."

"Not to fear, babies. I personally scraped it off."

I shifted nervously back and forth, pulling down on my *South Park* nightshirt. I stared at my sexy classmate — my body alive with his presence. I was totally embarrassed to be dressed for bed in front of a classmate. I fumbled with the envelope as he stepped into the foyer. He gazed at my legs while holding the hot pizza.

"We don't usually answer the door like this," Jazzy said, twirling her hair.

"Then it's my lucky night," he said to me with a coy glint in his eyes.

I was startled and dropped the money.

"Let me get that," he said, bending down. I kept my eyes on the floor as we scrambled to collect the bills.

"You're in my math class," Eddie said to me. "I knew you looked familiar. You're the one who never says anything."

I couldn't believe he had ever noticed me, that anyone had noticed me!

I scrambled to my feet and gave Eddie both twenties.

"Keep the change," I stammered.

He squeezed the bills in his hand. Then he gave me a huge smile and a sexy wink.

"See ya 'round, babies. Next time remember to wear a robe. Some of these delivery guys might get the wrong idea."

I watched him walk to his truck.

"He's hotter than that pizza!" Jazzy exclaimed. "He loves you, he totally loves you!"

I looked at my empty, trembling hands. "Oh no! I screwed up!"

"You'll be screwing him, girl! Did you see how he eyeballed you just before he left? He totally digs you!"

"He better dig me—I just gave him a twenty-five-dollar tip. And I forgot to use the coupon!"

That hefty tip landed me a date with Eddie.

I didn't dare make eye contact with him as I sat with my head in my notebook in Geometry class. But out of the corner of my eye I peeked up and could see how much more attractive he looked without his Pizza Town uniform on. I also noticed him glancing back at me, his blond hair flopping in his face. I shifted uneasily in my chair. For the first time Eddie was paying attention in Geometry—he was paying attention to me.

What was he thinking? I wondered. "She's so in love with me that she forgot the price of pizza and gave me all her money." Or, "She wants me so bad she tried to seduce me with a large tip." Or, "She obviously isn't learning anything in math—she can't even figure out how much a pizza costs!"

When the bell finally rang, I scooted out of class like a track star. Eddie grabbed his notebooks and followed after me.

"There's a party Saturday," he said, his green eyes piercing through me. He handed me a piece of paper ripped from his spiral binder. "I'll be there," he continued, with a wink. "Here's the address."

That was a date with Eddie. No flowers, no movie, no dinner. No seductive invitation, no "What's your number? I'll pick you up at seven." A date with Eddie meant a parentless house, grunger friends, booze. But I didn't care. Although I hadn't really ever noticed Eddie before, I now found myself strangely attracted to him. He was tempting, even in his bright red chinos and Pizza Town hat, and I'd go anywhere he wanted.

I hated parties, and despite Eddie's invitation I probably wouldn't have gone without Jazzy. Who would I talk to when I arrived? What would I say? What would people think of me? I preferred a rental movie night with Jazzy. We could scream and laugh and be our goofy selves. Parties were so painfully awkward. Hanging out with a bunch of drunken snobs who wouldn't talk to me during the middle of the week, let alone the weekend—it was just another place I didn't belong.

We arrived fashionably late in our party outfits—tight flowery tops and lots of beaded jewelry, Jazzy sporting a pastel blue headband over her bleached-blond hair and I wearing red heart barrettes in my orange hair. Smoke filled the dark foyer, and the pulsing beat of the Mojo Monsters echoed off the walls. Couples sat on long leather couches in the living room, drinking beer.

Eddie was nowhere to be found, so I sat on the edge of the sofa next to the TV, while Jazzy scoured the house. Jelly Bean was hosting *Saturday Night Live*. I escaped into the show, ignoring the critical glances of my schoolmates.

Gavin wouldn't act like these idiots, I thought. He wouldn't ignore a girl sitting alone. Then out of the corner of my eye I saw a jet-black-haired guy in a leather jacket coming down the stairs. Gavin! My heart sank. And I'm sitting here alone. Watching TV at a party. He'll see me and think I'm a total loser geek. I tried to find someone to talk to, but everyone around me was making out. I cringed.

But when he turned his face toward me I saw it wasn't Gavin after all. How could I have mistaken this disheveled loser for my passion, my heartthrob, my major crush, my knight in shining Calvins? Maybe it was the dim lighting or maybe I needed glasses. I breathed a sigh of relief. Because as exciting as it would be to see him on a weekend and get smile number eight, how could I bear to watch him glued all night to Stinkface's pouty lips?

"These are for you," Gavin said, handing me flowers as I opened my front door. He beamed a huge smile, smile

number eight with an exclamation point, his perfect teeth twinkling.

"Pink roses, my favorite!" I said, taking the flowers.

"I've been thinking about you all day," he confessed.

The sexual tension between us swelled to a peak; he kissed me on the cheek. His lips felt warm against my flesh.

He grabbed my hand and led me to his sparkling blue Volvo. "I got it waxed just for you!" he announced.

He squeezed my hand as we walked up the drive to the party. "I've seen you in the hall all these months. I tried to get you out of mind but I just couldn't!"

"Hey, Gavin!" Sam Chapman yelled as we entered the house.

"Hey, dude, this is my girlfriend, Trixie. Isn't she ravishing?"

"Yeah, man, she rocks!"

"Pleasure to meet you," I said, like a queen.

"The pleasure is mine!" He bent over and kissed my hand.

Our attention was drawn to a timid girl sitting alone on the edge of the sofa watching Saturday Night Live.

"I can't believe that!" Gavin said. "Her best friend is probably looking around for the doofus that invited her because she's too shy to ask herself. Guys should never treat girls that way."

★ ★ ★

"I've found him!" Jazzy screamed, grabbing me by the arm.

"Gavin?"

"Gavin? Eddie! Why aren't you mingling?"

"I was watching Jelly Bean."

"This is a party, Trix. We don't have to watch TV tonight!" Jazzy dragged me toward the kitchen.

"What if Eddie doesn't remember inviting me? What if he's with another girl?"

"Don't be so paranoid or I'll send you to my therapist!"

Several grungers were hanging out by the sink. Eddie was standing in front of the open refrigerator as if it was a sacred altar.

Jazlyn coughed loudly until he turned around. But he didn't smile and rush over to me and introduce me to his friends. He just gazed at us with an expression that said, "Why aren't you girls in the living room watching *Saturday Night Live?*"

I died inside. "We must have the wrong party!" I blurted out. "I was supposed to meet this totally cool guy. But I guess he's out delivering pizzas."

Eddie's friends laughed. Jazzy's jaw dropped to the floor. Eddie grinned from ear to ear.

"Hey, wait, baby!" he called, following me. He grabbed my shoulder and I instantly melted. "You want a beer?"

He took me by the hand and led me back through the kitchen, past Jazzy, who was cozily talking to one of his friends, and out onto the porch.

"Bud or Miller?" he asked, reaching into the cooler.

"No thanks, I'm in recovery," I joked.

But Eddie didn't get it. "That's cool, you just don't seem like a twelve-stepper."

"I took the Cliffs Notes version. There are only three steps and no meetings. Just a phone call."

Eddie's curiosity was as limited as his sense of humor, and he merely gave me a blank look. He opened a bottle for himself and took a long swig. Then he pulled me close. I was shocked by his sudden affection. His body was amazingly strong for someone with no visible muscles. He seemed very confident as he gazed deep into my eyes and kissed me slowly on the mouth.

It was like kissing a pizza. With extra sauce and spicy peppers and even forbidden cheese. I could feel the cold bottle against my back as he put his arms around my waist. We stood against the brick wall, kissing and touching, getting to know the geometry of each other's bodies as we never could in class.

"I always thought you were hot," he said, stopping for another swig of beer.

"I always liked the back of your head."

He laughed. Eddie Abels laughed at my joke!

Excitement ran through my bones.

"I wanted to thank you."

"Thank me?" I asked, puzzled.

"You know, for the major tip," he said. "It was very daring. It's always the quiet ones."

"So that's why I'm here?"

"No, that's why *I'm* here. I'm supposed to be working, but I asked for the night off."

He squeezed me back against the wall and kissed me slowly. It was like one of my fantasies. This couldn't really be happening to me.

"I'll pay you back . . . in slow installments," he said as he untucked my shirt and caressed the small of my back. His bony fingers moved up my naked skin, one vertebra at a time, until they reached my bra strap.

Just then Jazzy came out. "Trixie! We have to go!"

This was the first party I'd ever enjoyed, and we had to leave early.

"My mom paged me. Her car broke down, and I need to pick her up," Jazzy explained, as Eddie continued to kiss me. "Unless Eddie can take you home."

"I'm crashing here tonight," Eddie said, breaking away. "But there's plenty of room for two on the floor, baby."

"I didn't bring my sleeping bag," I said.

"Pizza Town is closed for the night!" Jazzy insisted,

grabbing my hand and leading me safely away.

"I thought you didn't have morals," I told her.

"I don't, but you do!"

Jazzy and I screamed as we ran across the lawn to her car. "I think his friend Ricky likes me!" she confessed. "And you and Eddie were having a total makeout festival! We have boyfriends!"

I glowed in the car, wondering what a thirty-dollar tip would bring.

A date with Eddie soon became a Friday night delivery ride around the city in his pizza truck. Sandwiched under large hot pizzas and cold two-liter bottles of Pepsi, I sucked in my gut for several hours and took home tiny bruises from the bottles thumping against my legs. But I was too happy to complain.

Heavy metal rocked through the speakers those nights. From inside his truck I watched Eddie confidently walk up the long paths to his customers' houses. "They're always happy to see me," he would say. "It's like delivering flowers, only they get to eat them." But Eddie always moaned about how he wanted to be doing something else. He had bigger dreams than this. "I want to own Pizza Town!"

Sarge and Dad liked Eddie because "He has a job!" I was allowed out with him once a week, and he was required to drive me safely home immediately after his shift. Each Friday before taking me home, however, he would park at the lakeshore. Free of delivery boxes, we had room to snuggle. Then around twelve thirty he pulled into my driveway and gave me a long kiss good night. I fell asleep peacefully tucked in my bed. A reminder of the evening etched in my flesh and hair, the scent of edible Eddie—pizza sauce and melted cheese.

"I have to make a quick stop; it'll only be a minute," Eddie said one night at the end of an exhausting evening of deliveries. "You can even carry the box."

Eddie had never asked me to carry the box before, which may not sound like a big deal, but for Eddie it was like asking a girl to wear his class ring. But more important than the honor was the chance to finally get out of the truck.

Eddie pulled into Chaplin's, the neighborhood comedy club.

I had always wanted to enter Chaplin's, but audience members had to be at least eighteen. But here I was, with a ticket in the shape of a pizza.

My eyes lit up when I saw the bright black-and-white fluorescent sign in the shape of a bowler hat and cane. I had always wondered what Chaplin's looked like inside.

Eddie took out a large pizza from the back. He then

threw a brown leather jacket over his Pizza Town shirt. "I hate going in here dressed like a pizza jerk," he explained. "The comics heckle me to death."

"What about me? Can I heckle you?" I asked coyly.

"It would be a dream come true, baby!"

The front door opened into a world I had only dreamed of. What stood before me was an entranceway filled with fame—black-and-white glossy framed head shots of famous comedians, adorned with signatures and funny comments. I was walking down the same black-tiled road that they had once taken. At the end of the corridor, beyond the ticket window and a small bar, stood a mysterious closed door from which spilled out the one sound I loved above all others—laughter.

"Eddie, I could smell you coming," the turtlenecked bartender said.

"Pepperoni smells better than vodka, Jack."

"Yeah, but vodka gets better tips."

"But with pizza you remember who you're waking up with."

"By the looks of it, you're doing okay, kid," Jack said, scrutinizing me. Normally I would have been upset at the lewd comment, but my eyes and ears were absorbing this new world. My gaze was glued to the closed theater door that held that new world inside, with laughter escaping. What lay beyond it?

"Jack, this is Trixie."

"Hey, Trixie," Jack said.

"Uh . . . hey, John, nice to meet you," I blurted out, still in my trance.

"Ben inside?" Eddie asked.

"Sure. Ask him to save me a slice."

"I'll try. C'mon," Eddie said to me. "And don't tilt the pizza."

But I was overwhelmed and handed over the box. "I have to go to the bathroom!" I wanted to compose myself. I felt as if I was about to perform.

I checked myself in the dingy bathroom mirror. "Makeup's okay; Piña Colada Passion lipstick needs a refresher . . . and the hair! Needs a major brush!"

My tiny purse was full of everything I could possibly need—quarters, a tampon, a purple marker, a grape Charms Blow Pop, three Starlite mints, a set of house keys, notes from Jazzy, a miniversion of my comedy notebook. But most importantly, one purple purse-sized Goody brush. I combed out my hair and fluffed it up with the hand dryer, wondering how many famous people had used this sink. Rosie? Roseanne? RuPaul?

I squeezed the hairbrush and saw the crowd smiling back in the mirror. "Good evening, ladies and gentleman," I said out loud. "It's great to be back here at Chaplin's. News flash—I have a boyfriend now. He

31

delivers pizza. But sometimes he gets confused when he drops me off after a date. He charges me a dollar-fifty for delivery!"

Suddenly an older woman was standing behind me, staring at me like she just stepped into a nuthouse. She quickly ran into a stall. Embarrassed, I threw the brush into my purse and flew out of the bathroom.

Eddie was not in the hallway.

I grabbed the long golden knobs of the theater doors and slowly pulled them open.

Suddenly my black-and-white world turned into Technicolor. I felt like a child at Disney World, a quarterback at the Super Bowl, an astronaut who landed on the moon.

All right, it was a dump. A tiny room with unvarnished floors, rickety wooden tables without tablecloths, and a cramped stage without curtains. In my eyes it was Oz.

A wiry man wearing a red bow tie and blue jeans stood onstage not forty feet away, holding a beer bottle in his hand, leaning against the microphone stand. I didn't even hear his jokes, I was so overwhelmed to be so close to a real comedian.

"Hey, baby! Over here," a voice whispered out of the darkness.

Eddie was sitting at a back table with a guy in jeans and a flashy rayon shirt.

"Trixie, this is my brother, Ben."

"Nice to meet you," I said, sitting in the chair next to Eddie. I didn't take my eyes off the comedian.

"I hope he's not driving you around the city all night instead of taking you to a movie," Ben said.

"Hey, anyone can see a movie. Want a slice of pizza, baby?"

"No thanks, it has cheese," I said, looking at the stage.

"This guy's good. I've seen him before. He's from Kentucky."

I was glued to the comedian, who appeared more comfortable onstage than I was when I woke up in the morning in my own bed. The audience laughed at a joke about a cow that he'd invited to the prom.

"I guess this beats sitting in the front seat of the truck!" Eddie whispered.

"You never told me your brother worked here," I whispered.

"He's the assistant manager. I give him free pizzas and he gives me free laughs."

Eddie's pager beeped. "Gotta get back to work," he said, squinting at the number. But then he saw the disappointment in my face—as if I was a toddler and playtime was over.

"That's the life when you date a pizza driver. Always on call," Ben philosophized.

Eddie got up. "You can stay here."

"I can?"

"This is funnier than someone's driveway."

I was surprised at his nonchalant attitude.

"Ben can give you a lift home."

"Actually, I can walk home," I offered.

"I think I can handle the door-to-door thing," Ben joked.

"Cool," Eddie said without a hint of jealousy. "See you later, Trixster." He stepped over and gave me a saucy kiss.

I loved Eddie at that moment. Not as a boyfriend, but as a friend. Loved him for exactly who he was, because any other guy would have insisted that I stick to his side and prevented me from hanging out alone in a dark club, would not have trusted his single brother to drive me home.

"I've got one last joke before I head outa here," the comedian said as he stubbed out his cigarette in his empty glass.

Sadly my dream was ending too soon. In a few minutes the club would be empty, couples giggling and retelling the jokes as they walked to their cars. I would have to go home as well and face an interrogation and possible court-martial for breaking curfew. But that was a small price to pay for a few moments in Oz.

★ ★ ★

On the way home that night Ben told me he could get me into Chaplin's for free whenever he was working the door. When he pulled into my driveway, I turned to him and said, as if I was making a vow, "I'm going to work there someday."

He offered to get me a job waiting tables. "No," I declared. "I mean onstage."

That summer I took Ben up on his offer and went to Chaplin's every chance I got. Sarge agreed to let me walk the two blocks to the club myself. But my dad always picked me up, waiting in the lobby, eating peanuts from the bar and reading *Sports Illustrated*. I felt like a pre-schooler as he chauffeured me home in our white Camry.

I didn't see much of Eddie anymore except when he came to the club with pizza. We remained good friends, and sometimes he remembered to bring me a small veggie without cheese.

MY WORST NIGHTMARE

☆

"Trix, you've gotta decide on Talent Night now!" Jazzy urged as she passed me the sign-up sheet in Drama class.

Despite my dream of performing at Chaplin's, the thought of actually being alone onstage at Talent Night was my worst nightmare. It was one thing to stand in front of a mirror in my comfortable bedroom, or to sit at a darkened table at Chaplin's, but it was quite another thing to perform alone on an enormous stage in front of hundreds of staring faces.

"I finally came up with a fab idea," Jazzy said. "I'm going to whistle the theme song from the *Andy Griffith Show*!"

"I don't think anyone's ever done that at Mason High," I said flatly. I looked down at my copy of *King Lear*.

"You mean it's been done at other schools? Do you know how long it took me to think of that?" And seeing the *King Lear*, she wrote down, "Shakespearean monologue."

"I'm not looking for anyone to sing all of *Les Mis*," Mr. Janson declared, leaning on his desk, "but you have to do more than state your name. No less than three minutes and no more than five. We may discover the next Streisand or Brando. All I ask is that you remember me when you accept your Oscar."

What if I sang "Happy Birthday" off-key? What if my Shakespearean soliloquy sounded as dead as the old bard himself, and I humiliated myself in front of all the teachers, parents, jocks, snobs, coolheads? And Gavin! The terror sent my heart leaping up out of my chest, out through my throat, and pounding down the hallway.

"I should have picked Sociology instead of Drama," I mumbled, staring at the sign-up sheet. "Maybe Janson will accept a written essay!" I pressed the pen against my lips. "On the other hand . . . ," and I scribbled on the line beside my name.

"I knew you'd come around. Let me see!"

"I can't believe I didn't think of it sooner!"

Jazlyn's mouth hung open. "'A reading from the diary of Jazlyn Peters.' You traitor! You're still trying to get me back for the time I called you Shrimp!" She paused, confused. "But you've never seen my diary!"

"I have too!"

"You sneak! I'll rehide it."

"I'll refind it!"

"I'll destroy it!"

"I'll speak from memory," I threatened.

Jazlyn quickly snatched back the sign-up sheet, crossed out my entry, and passed it across to Carl, a computer nerd.

"I knew you'd see it my way," I said.

"What's all that commotion?" Mr. Janson asked. "If you're truly having a difficult time thinking of something to perform, Ms. Shapiro, I have a million ideas begging to be shown to adoring eyes."

I hid behind *King Lear* propped open in front of me and doodled a picture of Mr. Janson in a Dorothy costume, complete with red ruby slippers. "Remember, people, this is a performance class, and if you don't have the passion to perform, you can take an F and be an usher."

An usher? I imagined tearing Gavin and Stinkface's tickets, leading them to their seats, dusting off their chairs like a servant.

"Ms. Peters, I see you've written 'Shakespearean monologue,'" Mr. Janson said, glancing at the sign-up sheet. "I must say, Jazzy, I'm quite impressed. Which one of the Bard's old standards will you be bringing to life?"

Jazzy proudly sat up. "*Romeo and Juliet*. I'll be doing Juliet's balcony speech to a cardboard cutout of Leonardo DiCaprio!"

The class snickered and rolled their eyes. Mr. Janson

looked off dreamily into the distance and, with a wicked smile, exclaimed, "Brilliant!" He looked back at the list. "Let's see, we have Mr. Reidel singing 'Tonight' from *West Side Story* and Mr. Davis reading Edgar Allan Poe's 'The Raven.'"

I knew I must make a decision now—take home a talent show program with my name on it, or an usher's badge with my name on it. "As for you, Ms. Shapiro, I'm very impressed!"

I was puzzled. Impressed with what? I hadn't written anything but the Jazlyn diary joke. And Jazzy had crossed it out—or had she written something over it?

"Class—Trixie Shapiro will be performing stand-up comedy!"

I died. Stand-up comedy! Terror shot through my veins. Of course comedy was my dream, but performing for Snoopy and Curious George is a lot different from performing for real classmates. Stuffed animals sit obediently with frozen smiles; classmates throw spitballs.

I turned to my former best friend, who was hiding behind *King Lear*. The whole class viewed me with shock and disbelief. They couldn't believe the quiet girl in the last row would have the guts to do stand-up. It would be a feat more daring than belly button piercing, bungee jumping, or bringing a number three pencil on the day of an exam.

★ ★ ★

"I can't believe you signed me up for stand-up!" I shouted as we walked to Jazzy's car after school. "I'm totally freaking out! My ulcer is acting up, and I don't even have an ulcer."

"You'll be fabulous," Jazzy said nonchalantly. "You can put your hair in pigtails and put on those funny purple house shoes with the fuzzy pom-poms. You won't have to say a word."

"Stand-up isn't like Shakespeare. What if they don't laugh? I'll be the first person to perform stand-up tragedy."

"Look, Trix, you've always told me you want to be a comedian."

"Duh! But I'm still in high school, Jazz. This isn't as simple as taking drama class and performing scenes from A *Streetcar Named Desire*. First of all, I'll be writing my own jokes. And I won't have actors to react to. Performing comedy is really hard when no one is laughing."

"You may hate my guts now, but when you're on the *Douglas Douglas Show*, you'll thank me! Then you'll forget me. But I'm willing to sacrifice our friendship for your dream."

I winced. "I don't think you see the magnitude of this. This isn't like lip-synching 'Fernando' at a slumber party. This is like standing naked in front of the whole entire school. Including Gavin!"

"Yes, and you'll make him realize there's more to life than plastic boobs and plastic personalities. And besides, did you notice how the class reacted? They envy you! Those losers could never even dream of being so courageous. You'll finally show them what 'bush girls' are all about."

"That we're more than losers?"

"We aren't losers! It's just that everyone else is so three years ago—they haven't caught up to us to know how hip and truly rockin' we are!"

"I'm glad one of us has high self-esteem."

"Tell that to my therapist!"

Just then Ricky caught up with us and gave Jazzy a slow kiss.

"I guess that also helps," I said, looking away.

"I heard that our cute little Trixie is going to do stand-up," Ricky said, pulling away from Jazzy and turning to me. "That's fab . . . that takes guts! Not like professing your love to a cardboard movie star," he added.

Jazzy gave him a dirty look in return.

COMEDY AND TRAGEDY

☆

"I love you," Jazzy said, kissing Leonardo DiCaprio on the mouth. "Isn't he gorgeous?" she then asked me. The poster of the actor, freshly glued to thick cardboard, was leaning against Jazzy's dresser. "Why don't you borrow him? He might cheer you up."

"I need a cardboard Jelly Bean. Then I could hide behind it to recite my stupid jokes. No one would dare throw textbooks at Jelly."

"No one's going to throw anything at you but money! And underwear—Gavin Baldwin's Joe Boxers. O Leonardo, Leonardo, wherefore art thou Leonardo?" Jazzy proclaimed, balancing on her wicker chair. "Deny thy father and refuse thy fame!"

"Fame? That's not the way it goes."

"It's a whole metaphor thing, don't you see?" she declared wildly.

"Shakespeare is having a cow right now!" I said, rolling my eyes.

"Your turn!" Jazzy exclaimed, jumping off the chair.

"No way."

"If you can't perform in front of your best friend, how can you perform in front of the whole school?"

"Exactly!"

"We crack each other up all the time! You're always goofing around. You should be used to this."

"But it's not the same. I'll be up there alone."

"We'll all be up there alone."

"You have Leo." I put my hand to my forehead. "My head feels warm. Do you think I have a fever?"

"I'm hot too. It's Leo's scorching image. I'll put him in the closet."

"No, I really think I'm sick."

"Just take a deep breath and read from your comedy notebook. I promise I won't laugh," Jazzy said, and laughed out loud. "Did you get that, Trix? That was a joke! Hey, I should be the one doing the comedy!"

"Yeah, you should."

"No one said this stuff is easy," she said, suddenly serious. "Could Sam Chapman do stand-up? He tells jokes in class, but he does it just to get out of trouble, not to entertain. He'd freeze onstage. No one would laugh. We'll get you drunk!"

"I'll need more than liquor!"

"I'll see what I can do, but right now try it one time for me."

I looked at my notebook and then at my watch. "Rancid! It's six fifteen. Sarge will kill me. I told her I'd be home to set the table."

"But I need to practice!"

"Jazz, I'll be grounded."

"There's your excuse. You can tell Janson you can't perform 'cause you're grounded!"

I looked at my best friend. And slowly a wicked grin overcame me.

The next night I fiddled with my straw as I sat alone at my usual table, hidden by the dim lights and thick smoke that hung over the audience at Chaplin's.

But as I watched the opener dying, I thought: I can do that. I can stand onstage and not be funny! But standing up in front of Gavin and the whole school and not being funny was another thing. I looked at my watch. 9:45. 10:05. 10:30.

Dad was in Houston on business, so I told Sarge I'd get a ride with Ben, knowing he would be one of the last to leave.

"Man, I'm sorry, it's so late," Ben said, cutting off the club lights. "I hope Sergeant doesn't have a fit!"

"I hope she does," I said with a wink.

But my plan had a fatal flaw. Sarge's punishment wasn't grounding me from Talent Night after all—her punishment was chaperoning me to Janson's Rehearsal Night!

I insisted Sarge sit quietly in the back of the auditorium. I ignored her and sat as far away from her as I could, slunk down in the front row next to Jazzy.

Mr. Janson talked to the accompanist who sat at his piano stage left while seventeen drama students giggled, gossiped, and chatted on cell phones, breaking up the nervous tension.

"Settle down," Janson finally commanded, taking center stage. "Since we only have one rehearsal, and this is the first time Roger is here to learn the musical accompaniment, we'll run all musical numbers in order first."

"Awh man!" one student whined. "I'm not even warmed up!"

"This sucks," I complained to Jazzy. "We'll have to wait hours before we get our turn over with!"

I was right. If Rehearsal Night was any indication of Talent Night, audience members would be fleeing toward the exits—it was a disorganized, off-key mess. Ten students were performing musical numbers, and more than half of them had to run through their songs at least three times.

"When will you be going on?" Sarge abruptly interrogated me, nudging my arm while Harold Quimby warbled through "Music of the Night."

"Shh, Ma! Didn't you hear Mr. Janson? He's running musical numbers first."

"I wanted to go to the ladies' room and I don't want to miss your routine."

"Unless you're going back home to use the toilet, you won't miss a thing! It'll be more than an hour."

"Do you kids have vending machines here?" she asked, removing my backpack from the seat next to me and stuffing herself into the chair. "I need a nosh."

"Down the hall," I said, pointing, but not making eye contact. "And around the corner, out the steps, and down the block."

"Do you want something?" she asked, ignoring my comment. "You must be starved."

"Ma! Everyone's looking!"

"Jazzy, would you like a treat?" she asked, leaning over me.

"No thanks, Mrs. Shapiro. My stomach is in knots!"

"Shhh!" I sternly whispered. "Molly is singing. You're embarrassing me."

"That's what mothers are for!" she retorted, and walked up the aisle.

"This is torture," I whispered to Jazzy.

We chatted, slept, and doodled as the hours dragged on. I painted my nails blue and Jazzy re-applied eye shadow.

"Okay, guys!" Janson said anxiously after the epic musical numbers were over. "We're running out of time. We'll do tops and bottoms. That means we'll run the show in order, but only for lighting cues. Be ready on deck backstage. When lights go up, hit your mark, say your first line, then jump to your closing line, applause-applause from the audience, lights out, and make your way offstage!"

"Is he kidding?" I said, as we quickly stashed our accessories.

"But Mr. Janson," Jazzy called, her hand raised wildly. "Some of us haven't performed yet!"

"I know, I'm sorry, but that's all we'll have time for tonight. It's almost eleven o'clock."

We anxiously waited backstage for our turn. Jazzy dragged Leo backstage, tired and frustrated. "It's a blessing," I tried to reassure her. "Now we only have to perform once!"

"I didn't think of it that way," she said, relieved. "Now go! It's your turn."

I hit my mark.

I'd never stood on Mason's stage. It felt huge and engulfing. I could barely make out the empty seats with the blinding lights. I finally held a real microphone in my hand.

"Say your line!" Mr. Janson called.

"Oh yeah . . ." My voice echoed throughout the auditorium. "I loathe high school," I began. "I'm unbearably shy—afraid to speak up in—"

"Cut!" he admonished me.

I stopped mid–punch line. "Did I do something wrong?"

"Yes, you're supposed to jump to your last line, Trixie! We have six other performers to get through. We'll have to take out a school levy for the electricity we've been running tonight!"

That was my rehearsal.

"Thank you very much," I said, reluctantly jumping to the end of my routine, replacing the microphone in its stand. I bowed.

"Lights out! Applause, applause," Janson called to the light board operator.

The stage went pitch-black. I struggled slowly in the darkness, afraid I might trip over the mike cord or fall off the stage.

The lights came on and I was still fumbling through the red curtain.

"Hold it, Harold!" Mr. Janson called, waving Harold offstage as he began entering from stage right. "Trixie! What are you still doing onstage?"

"My curtain call?" I asked.

The students all laughed from backstage. Some even

applauded. I bowed and quickly ran off.

"Save your jokes for tomorrow please, Ms. Shapiro," Janson reprimanded me.

Jazzy and I were gathering our backpacks when I heard a familiar voice call from the back of the auditorium.

"Excuse me, Mr. Janson!"

"Uh-oh!" Jazzy said, clutching Leonardo.

"Tell me she doesn't want to sing tomorrow too!"

"No, I think she's pissed!" Jazzy whispered.

I thought the punishment was over, but I guess it had just begun.

Sarge stormed down the auditorium aisle and brazenly approached Mr. Janson, who was putting papers in his duffel bag. Students who were leaving hung back, watching.

"You mean to tell me that I sat through three hours of music rehearsal and 'lights up, lights down,' and I didn't get to watch my own child run through her performance even one time?"

"Ma!"

"I'm sorry, Mrs. Shapiro. I had no idea we'd run over schedule. This year's show had more musical numbers than last year's."

"But the dramatic and comedic pieces deserve attention too."

"You're right, but I feel it's more important the kids get

a good night's rest for the show tomorrow."

"She forgot to take her Prozac," I whispered to some of the students that had gathered.

But Sarge ignored my comment. "How is she supposed to get a good grade if she isn't prepared?"

"She's going through menopause," I whispered. "Mood swings!"

"Listen, Mr. Janson—," she continued.

"I'll let her and the others have a few minutes onstage before the show. Don't worry, Mrs. Shapiro. I have the utmost confidence that Trixie will be great tomorrow."

"Really, you think she's talented?"

"Ma! The school is closing!"

"First rate," Mr. Janson said offhandedly, zipping his duffel bag.

"Did you hear that, Trixie? He said my baby's so good she doesn't need rehearsal," she said, patting me on the back like I was one of her third-graders.

"I think she deserves an A for her performance!" I whispered to Mr. Janson, as Jazzy and I followed Sarge out.

When I got home, I called Sid on his cell phone.

"Trixie? I can't hear you," he shouted over the sounds of kids partying and loud music. "Hey, dudes—I'm trying to talk to my sis!"

"Sid?"

"Let me go outside," he said.

"I'd like your advice," I began.

"You want to know what kids wear to a Phish concert?"

"No—"

"Where to get a fake ID?"

"Listen—"

"How to cut class?"

"Exactly!"

"You've had perfect attendance since kindergarten." He laughed. "Let me guess. Talent Night?"

"Sarge told you?"

"Actually I read it in USA *Today*."

"But I'm freaking out. I can't do it!"

"You'll rock!" he exclaimed. "You're a natural."

"But this is the first time I'll be performing without you!"

"Well, it's about time."

"But Sid—"

"Listen. Just imagine I'm onstage with you."

"Could you be?" I begged.

"No, but I'll be in the audience."

The audience! The thought of my brother grinning at me in the front row only terrified me further. "Oh, Sid, you can't!"

"I wouldn't miss it for the world."

"Don't you have a wet T-shirt contest to judge or something?"

"I cleared my schedule for you, Shrimp."

"But you're allergic to school," I reminded him. "I bet you don't even know where Mason's auditorium is."

"Of course I do. I used to sneak a smoke in the prop room. So no fear, girl. This is one class project I'm not going to miss."

Before going to bed, I scrutinized myself in the mirror, the round hairbrush held tightly in one hand, the stuffed animals in their places. I felt a burst of confidence.

"I loathe high school," I began for the seventeenth time. But then reality hit me as I noticed the drooping eyes reflected in the mirror.

What if I failed in front of the whole school?

I jumped on my bed and crawled under the covers fully clothed, my brush still clutched in my hand. I had nineteen hours to catch the flu.

"I'm so totally excited!" Jazzy screamed as she drove me to school the next morning. "The best part will be the party afterward. We'll be the stars—everyone will want to hang with us—especially with you, 'cause you have the best act!"

"You haven't even see it!"

"But all the other acts tanked at rehearsal!"

"I just hope I'm still breathing afterward!"

"We'll get A pluses from Janson and party with Ricky and Gavin."

"Don't say Gavin! Why did we take this class anyway?"

"We thought it would be fun," Jazzy answered.

"Boy, were we wrong," we both said in unison.

At 10:55 I passed Gavin in the hallway. But today I kept my eyes on the floor, afraid to make eye contact, afraid to draw attention to myself. So when he stepped toward me for the first time ever, I ignored him like a coward and hurried to class.

The closed curtains concealed the arriving crowd—a small one, I hoped. We couldn't hear them for all the noise backstage. Mr. Janson was rushing around trying to create some order out of all our chaos.

I paced in the wings, wearing a silky dark blue dress, black tights, and black high heels. Why didn't I wear high tops and a pair of shorts? I wondered, as I slid on a Talent Night program that was lying on the floor.

"People, get in your places," Mr. Janson commanded. "Remember the running order, remember to project, and most importantly, remember me when you're famous!"

"I need oxygen!" I said to Jazzy.

Jazzy's face was pale as she held on tightly to her cardboard Leo.

I hadn't ever seen Jazzy afraid of anything. I had to be strong for her. "Remember, we're bush people," I said, grabbing her hand. But our clasped hands were shaking. "We survived thorns and branches. Those people out there are just flowers in comparison."

"Thanks, Trix," Jazzy said, and squeezed me with all her might.

"Now I must be alone," I demanded. "We'll talk after the show." I needed to tune everyone out so I could run through my material. I wouldn't be able to relax until my performance was over. I sat curled up on a backstage chair, waiting forever for my name to be called, trying to convince myself I was being thrown into a bed of roses and not another thorn bush.

I tried to tune out a shrilling rendition of "Memory," a rap version of "Silent Night," and finally Jonathan Marks reading from *Othello*—my cue to go on. I watched him from the wings as I shook, paced, bit my nails, and jumped up and down. I didn't listen to a word of his speech. It was as if he was performing on speed.

Jonathan, the center on Mason's basketball team, was delivering the bard's words as if he was speaking against the shot clock. There was a round of applause and suddenly I heard, "For our next act, please welcome to the stage . . . Trixie Shapiro!"

I couldn't move — my feet were frozen.

"Where is she?" Janson whispered, peeking backstage. "Trixie, you're on!"

Jazzy ran over, waving her arms. "Trixie, it's your turn!"

I stared at her with wide ghostlike eyes. She pushed me onstage like a mother bird pushing her baby out of the nest. I walked forward, my knees wobbly, my hands sweaty. I picked up the mike from its stand and squeezed it like a pacifier.

I stood alone on the huge stage I had so often gazed at during study hall, in front of a sea of dark faces — all staring back at me. And not a Snoopy or Hello Kitty among them. No mirror to check myself in. No laugh track to spur me on.

The spotlight made me squint, but I also felt its warm glow. And with a sudden burst of confidence, I thought: This is the moment. I wasn't going to blow it — rather I was going to blow the audience away. Bring down the house, be the best performer Talent Night had ever seen. Show the snobs what I had dreamed of for so long—show the world.

When my eyes adjusted to the glare, I noticed a smiling Sergeant in the third row, her program clenched tightly in her hand. I saw Dad and Aunt Sylvia, beaming. And then I saw Sid—grinning at me just as I had imagined. I started to perspire. I looked toward the aisle and saw my Algebra 2 teacher, Mr. Benchley, staring right at me. I could barely make out cheerleaders still dressed from the game scattered around the theater, glaring. I fingered my hair with my free hand. Eddie was in the first row, left section, sitting with some of his friends from American History class. I started to gnaw on my bottom lip. I spotted Sam Chapman in an aisle seat reading his program. And then I saw Gavin. My hands began to shake and I tried to cover my nervous tension with a Cheshire cat grin.

Why was everyone I knew sitting so close to the stage? Why couldn't they have been farther back, blocked by the glare of the spotlight?

I felt like I had been standing up there forever.

Speak, you moron! Do it. Do it now! Get it over with. They'll laugh and you'll be able to get outa here. They can't see your shaking hands.

I took a deep breath.

Nothing. Blank. My brain was empty. The monologue, all the jokes I'd been practicing all my life were gone. Vanished. Sucked into a dark abyss.

If I could just remember one joke, it would bring the rest back.

I gazed at the balcony, as if my words were written on banners like "Go Mustangs" at a Mason High football game. I wrinkled my forehead, hoping to force my material out. My palms were so sweaty, the mike slipped in my hand. I couldn't believe this was happening. I couldn't remember a thing. I was dying in front of my family and the whole school. I looked at Sergeant.

Anything funny about Sergeant? I rattled my brain.

All of a sudden there wasn't anything funny about the woman whose smile was now turning into a nervous grin.

Dad! But Dad never says anything. I couldn't remember anything he had ever said!

Sid? He was no longer the only one in the family to suffer blackouts. Something about drugs . . . but what? What! I bit my fingernails. I felt like I was stuck in Jell-O.

If I could remember one joke anyone has ever told me . . .

Nothing.

My very first joke.

Emptiness.

One from a comedy album.

Blank.

A dirty limerick.

Nada.

Students were fanning themselves with their programs, shifting in their seats. I was really beginning to panic.

Okay, forget comedy!

Recite a nursery rhyme.

Zero.

If I could remember the song about the lamb that follows that girl . . . Maggie . . . Millie?

I could hear sounds of boredom in the audience—sighs, yawns, coughing.

Sing the national anthem. How does it go again?

A bumper sticker?

Nothing.

A license plate number.

Nothing.

My name—no, that's the one thing I wanted to forget.

Beads of sweat dripped down my forehead. I noticed students glancing around, heard programs rustling, audience members whispering. Were my five minutes up? I felt I'd been onstage for five years! I stared out into the audience. I melted from the heat of the spotlight. I squeezed the microphone, shaking and slipping in my sweaty hands and finally brought it up to my mouth.

"I have to go and throw up now! I forgot I was supposed to do that *before* I came onstage."

The crowd paused awkwardly for a second, then roared with laughter as I desperately escaped offstage.

BROKEN DREAMS

Sid found me hiding in the girls' bathroom after the show. I had hoped to wait until the whole school left, and then slip out unnoticed.

"Do you always use the girls' bathroom?" I asked, peeking out from the stall.

"It's a great place to meet chicks," he replied.

"I bombed!" I said, stepping out.

"You rocked," he lied, patting me on the arm.

"You must be having a flashback," I argued. "Maybe if the rest of the audience had been having hallucinations too, I would have gotten a standing ovation."

My brother laughed.

"Now why couldn't you have done that when I was up there?" I asked him.

Sid hugged me. Cigarette smoke and incense imbedded in his clothes made my eyes tear.

"Don't be upset," he comforted me, wiping my leaking eye with his sleeve.

Sid put his arm around me. In his big brother way, he

proudly escorted me to the car as tears continued to well up in my eyes. I didn't have the heart to tell Sid it was just that I needed a gas mask to be around him.

Sergeant and Dad tried to reassure me on the long ride home, while I slumped silently in the backseat. Aunt Sylvia thoughtfully added, "You looked so pretty onstage. So grown-up. You were much better than that girl who recited Shakespeare to the poster. She turned white as a ghost when it fell over on her."

"That's my best friend you're talking about!" I burst out. And then I remembered who had gotten me into this mess. I hadn't stayed to watch Jazzy's performance, or talked to her after the show. After my fiasco I had locked myself in a bathroom stall until Talent Night was over.

At home I immediately threw my stuffed animals into my closet, the Goody hairbrush into the garbage can, and the laugh track under the bed. I ripped Jelly Bean's poster from my wall.

Exhausted, I stared into my dreadful mirror like a wicked witch wondering who was the least funny of all. It was just a stupid dream. The only headlining I was capable of performing was at a carnival freak show. "Ladies and gentleman, you have just witnessed the Bearded Girl, the Mermaid Girl, and now we have for you live, straight from Amber Hills, the Loser Girl!"

I unscrewed the mirror from the door and put it in the closet with the rest of my dreams.

I didn't return to school the next day. Before Talent Night I'd had perfect attendance. Sergeant was beside herself, threatening to call Jazzy's therapist. Dad insisted on driving me to school, but first he had to get me out of bed. I told Sarge I wanted to be homeschooled. I would be sure to get high marks in Laundry 2 and American Vacuuming.

No longer dreaming about comic stardom, I fantasized about being an astronaut and living among aliens who'd never heard of Trixie Shapiro or Talent Night.

I was watching *Sunset Boulevard* one afternoon when the doorbell rang. I wasn't accepting calls or visits from Jazzy. But a man peered back at me from the other side of the peephole.

"Mr. Janson! What are you doing here?"

"Extreme actions call for extreme measures," he said.

"I was just watching *Sunset Boulevard* for the ninth time," I said, pausing the movie.

"Gloria Swanson gives the performance of a lifetime."

"Yeah, she really has it, doesn't she? Some are meant to perform, and some are meant to watch. Want a HoHo?"

"You must be really sick."

"Yeah. Monday I had the flu, Tuesday a stomachache, Wednesday a headache, Thursday a virus, and today the flu again. I don't blame you for failing me. I'm looking into transferring anyway. I've decided to go to technical school. I've given the matter a lot of thought and I realize high school is passé. All you get out of it is a periodic table and a prom. What can you do with that when you're thirty? I'm looking toward the future."

"And what would that be, Ms. Shapiro?"

"Refrigerator repair."

He tried to hold back a smile.

"Everyone has one. And the ice maker always goes on the fritz just before a party. That's when I come in. Only I'll wear a dress with a pink tool belt—not those horrible jeans those men wear that keep falling down when they bend over."

"It seems you've thought this through."

"I've liked refrigerators ever since I can remember."

"Jazzy explained that she signed you up for stand-up. She thought she was doing you a favor."

"Now audiences all over the world will get a favor—my early retirement!"

"She feels horrible."

"She can tell it to her therapist. I think she gets a discount if she goes over an hour."

"What would you say if I said I thought you were funny?"

"I'd say something I'm not supposed to say to a teacher."

"Three hundred people can't be wrong. Didn't you hear them laugh?"

"It was hard to hear them over the sound of my heels hitting the floor in flight. Besides, they were laughing at me, not with me."

"You accomplished the assignment. You were supposed to stand onstage alone for several minutes and hold the audience's attention. And since you chose stand-up—or since it was chosen for you—you wanted the audience to laugh. Which they did. I gave you an A."

"I don't deserve to pass, much less get an A. I didn't deserve that laugh!"

"You improvised a line that got you out of a desperate situation. Everyone is afraid to do what you did. To go onstage, to tell a joke. A lot of popular kids who think they own the world take my class. But they turn into big marshmallows when I ask them to perform in front of their peers. You have the dream and passion inside you, and you have guts. No one can take that away. Talent Night was your first experience, not your only experience. And if you always remember that you passed instead of failed, then you can look back on it with pride."

"I'll never look back on Talent Night with pride."

"Then look at your report card with pride."

The dark clouds that were hovering over my world started to drift away. I almost felt the sun peeking through.

"Thanks for coming over. I think my stomachache will go away now."

"Fabulous! But I do have just one request before I go."

"You changed your mind about that HoHo?"

"It's another assignment. But this one's just for you, strictly elective."

"Oh no," I cried, panic setting in, imagining another Talent Night just for me.

"I signed you up for Open Mike at Chaplin's."

I began to feel flu symptoms coming on again.

"Each amateur gets five minutes. These people have never been up on a stage before in their lives. You're farther along. You can use the material you were planning for Talent Night. You can even read your jokes from cards. There's no pressure. It'll be fun."

"But, I can't do this, don't you understand?"

"You can't *not* do this. I'll see you tomorrow night at Chaplin's. I'll sit in the back so I won't make you nervous," he said, letting himself out.

"Oh no," I sighed, feeling my forehead. "I think now I really do have a fever!"

OPEN MIKE

I crept into Chaplin's for the hundredth time, but tonight my stomach turned as I walked the hallway of fame—instead of being an audience member sitting safely behind an appetizer list and a haze of smoke, I would be a performer, alone onstage, delivering jokes, with a spotlight shining straight down on me.

"I'm here for Open Mike," I whispered to a chain-smoking woman checking off names on a sign-in sheet.

"Hi, I'm Joyce. Who are you, sweetie?"

"Trixie Shapiro."

"Shapiro . . . You'll be number seven. Do you know the rules?"

"You have rules?"

"No swearing, especially the F word. No more than five minutes onstage. Jimmy, the guy testing the mike, will shine a flashlight at four minutes so you can wrap it up. Gary," she added, waving to a guy in a red-flannel shirt, "is the emcee. Any questions?"

"Does he know CPR?"

"You'll be fine!"

"No F word and no more than five minutes," I repeated.

"And there's another rule. Have fun!"

Have fun? I only hoped it would be more fun than sitting in the dentist's chair.

I hung by myself at a darkened table while other would-be comics checked in. Where was Janson? I decided it was best for me not to look around for him. Anyone or anything could be a distraction to me. Hopefully he wouldn't show. He did say this was an elective. Maybe he elected to grade papers.

"Trixie," a deep voice called from behind me.

Startled, I quickly turned around. It was Ben. "I saw your name on the list," he said. "Cool!"

"You can't watch!" I demanded.

"Are you crazy?"

"You'll make me nervous. More nervous than I already am."

"You'll be fine."

"I'm not fine! Please!" I begged.

"Okay, girl, I'll slip in the back when I hear your name called. Want a drink?"

"How about a Coke and rum without the Coke?"

"How about a Coke and ice without the ice?"

"Who's the comedian?" I said. I sat down alone at my usual table in the back and began to pray.

★ ★ ★

The amateur comedians weren't nearly as funny, polished, or confident as the touring professionals I'd been watching at Chaplin's. They clutched the mike like a beer bottle, bringing it to their mouths then letting it dangle, slurring the punch lines—if there were any. Several participants told inside jokes to their friends in the audience, who laughed like crazy.

The Coke went right through me, so I made a bathroom run as comic number four left the stage.

I looked in the mirror and forced a smile. I had all my lines written on a tiny piece of paper hidden in my bra— just in case I blanked out. I fluffed my hair and said my first line. "Just have fun," I then reminded myself. "Fun—now that's the F word!"

I had one more chance to go to the bathroom, I thought, and headed back to the stall. My mind must have wandered and before I knew it, I had flushed down a whole roll of paper.

The toilet began to overflow! Great. I had just ruined Oz's plumbing.

Suddenly the ladies' room door opened. "You're on!" Ben scolded.

"But I—," I began.

"No time." He grabbed my arm and pulled me out into the theater as Gary said, "We have only one female

could have seen you. He'd have treated you to a free pizza!"

I was buzzing from the sudden attention. People noticing me? Talking to me? Complimenting me?

Suddenly Mr. Janson approached. I had forgotten all about him, and for a moment wondered why he was here.

"You were brilliant! Just brilliant," he exclaimed, hugging me.

"I passed?"

"Just remember me when you're on Comedy Central!" he exclaimed.

Gary closed the show after the final unbearable amateur, and the lights came up. I gathered my purse and jacket.

"You cracked me up!" the heckler said, shaking my hand.

"Thanks for coming!" I beamed.

Several of the other amateurs came over to me and we exchanged compliments. Finally a very unfunny doctor shook my hand.

"You were great," he said and shook my hand. His wife beamed and agreed. "You were delightful."

What could I say to him? I'm glad you have something to fall back on? Instead, I said, "Great job!" as I noticed a hipster picking up a leather jacket from a table in the back. A knockout was leaving his side and walking toward the doctor. No, it couldn't be. Stinkface?

The familiar blonde stormed around me and said, "See ya, Uncle Stevie," following the doctor and his wife out toward the lobby. I turned around. Now I could make out Gavin's face.

How could I have not noticed them before? They must have arrived when I was flooding the bathroom. I hoped Gavin wouldn't storm around me, so I could get smile number eight to cap off my most magical evening. But he didn't pass me; instead he walked right toward me.

"I thought you were awesome!" he said with smile number eight.

Despite years of my infatuation and seven prior smiles, Gavin Baldwin had never actually spoken to me.

Now I had stage fright. I couldn't even say thanks. I barely returned the smile.

"I didn't know you were so talented!"

"Yeah, I guess I can do more than walk and chew gum at the same time," I blurted out as if I were still onstage.

"Gavin, are you going to take me home? Or am I going to have to walk?" Stinkface called over impatiently.

"She's chewing gum," he whispered, "so I guess I

shouldn't let her walk. She's not that talented," he said with a wink, and was gone.

I was at a gala charity ball shimmering in a silver glit-ter dress, slow dancing with a tuxedoed Jerry Seinfeld when Eddie Murphy tapped his shoulder to cut in—

I heard a pounding at my door.

Jazzy barged into my room and blinded me by turning on the lights.

"Jazzy! How'd you get in here?"

"I had to hide inside a wooden horse!"

"But I was just about to dance with Eddie Murphy. Let me go back to sleep!"

"You can't! You have school and I have to talk to you."

"Aren't I mad at you?" I asked, pulling the covers over my head.

"I'm sorry about signing you up for stand-up at Talent Night," she apologized, pulling the covers down.

"You mean Fright Night! It was totally scary—I was totally scary!"

"You weren't scary—I was!" she said, plopping on the edge of my bed. "Leonardo came unglued and fell down on me. So there I was in front of the whole school with Leonardo DiCaprio lying on top of me!"

"Sounds like a dream come true!"

"Not when your mom is in the third row. I could hear everyone snickering. I've never been so totally embarrassed in my life."

"Aunt Sylvia thought it was funny."

"I'm the one who shouldn't have come back to school, Trix. Ricky thought my monologue was rancid! He kept saying at the party, 'Where's Trixie? She was hysterical!' He thought you planned your routine that way!"

"No way!"

"I talked to my therapist all week. She was the only one who'd listen to me—and I have to pay her!" She pulled at her beaded necklace. "Anyway, I don't care about that stupid night. I just want us to be best friends again."

"But I care about that night. I'll never forget it."

"I know. I'm so sorry! I thought I was doing you a favor—like Sid pushing you out from behind the couch. But I'll never put you in harm's way again."

"You promise?"

"I promise! I promise!"

"Well . . . okay."

"So we're bush girls again?"

"Really, Jazz . . . How can I go to school without you? Who will I eat lunch with? Who will I pass notes to?" I asked.

"Oh goody!" Jazzy screamed, squeezing me tightly. "I have a little present for you," she then said, opening her purse and handing me a bottle of nail polish.

"True Blue!" I said, reading the color. "Cool, Jazzy!"

"Now let's get to school," she said, fixing her hair in the mirror.

I scrounged for some clean school clothes. "I have the most amazing news to tell you in the car!"

"Is it blockbuster news?"

"Totally blockbuster! With paparazzi and autographs. It takes place at a comedy club and it stars me and . . . Gavin Baldwin!"

"Gavin!"

"He spoke to me! Finally, after a lifetime!"

"No way! What did he say?"

"Let me start from the beginning! He was wearing—"

"Wait, get dressed. Then you can tell me every juicy detail. I'll drive extra slow!"

The bell rang at 10:55, signaling freedom from my prison cell known as Anatomy. I was late getting out of class, cleaning up the glitter that had sprinkled out from one of Jazzy's notes. I was still reading it in the bustling hallway when someone grabbed me by the arm and the note fell to the floor.

"Hey, doofus! Look what you made me do!" I exclaimed. The note landed next to a combat boot, which was connected to blue jeans, and then an oversized rust sweater. . . .

"Gavin!" I exclaimed, breathless.

Was I dreaming? He was touching my arm! And what a firm hunkster grip he had! But why was he grabbing me?

Gavin bent down and picked up the note, like the gentleman I'd always dreamed he was.

I froze like a deer in headlights when he noticed its unmistakable contents spelled out in bold purple glitter:

T.S.

x

G.B.

Gavin looked at me with skeptical eyes.

"G . . . arth . . . Br . . . ooks. I love Garth Brooks!" I blurted out, grabbing the note.

"You don't look like the country music type."

"What type do I look like?" I asked.

He gazed at me, really stared at me—studied my bob-length orange hair pulled back in two orange flower barrettes, my dark eyes—and then glanced down to the nape of my neck. My skin flushed like I was in a steam room. I shifted in place, fingering my hair. And then he averted his eyes as if trying to find the right words.

The bell rang.

"You look like the Varicose Veins type," he said over the sounds of closing lockers and classroom doors. "I've got two tickets to their concert next week. Want to go?"

Did I want to go? Did I want a million dollars? Did I want my own HBO special?

"Sounds cool," I replied, trying to act nonchalant.

He smiled—number nine—and his blue eyes sparkled like the glitter on my note. "What's your number?"

"Of smiles?" I asked.

"Smiles?"

"Oh, of course!" I laughed, scribbling my telephone number on his spiral notebook, trying desperately to cover my faux pas.

"You are a funny girl," he said as he left.

Walking through the empty corridors, I floated to class on a Gavin Baldwin–shaped cloud.

But when I got there, instead of receiving congratulations for winning a date with Gavin Baldwin, I was met by the confused stare on my ignorant teacher's face.

"Can I help you?" he asked when I entered the room. "Are you lost?"

"Lost? I'm in your class!"

The students laughed.

"Oh," he said, squinting at me. "Then you're late."

Mr. Owens warned me if I was tardy again I would

receive a detention. I would stay after school every day just to have Gavin touch my arm again. And that afternoon I imagined all about the things he could do to get me suspended.

"This is like an episode of *Fantasy Island!*" Jazzy screamed to me in my celebrity-pasted bedroom later that night.

"I have nothing to wear! Absolutely nothing!" I screamed back, frantically throwing skirts, blouses, sweaters, and jackets on my bed. "He'll show up at my door and think he's at the Salvation Army!"

"Chill, Trix—we'll find you a dress," Jazzy said, weeding through the tossed clothes.

"But all I have is rags, and I just spent my allowance on Woody Allen DVDs. Do banks give out loans for dream dates?"

"I still can't believe you're going out with him!"

"I know, but I can't go if I have to wear this."

"Relax," Jazzy said, ignoring my angst. She held the framed photo of Gavin I had copied from last year's yearbook. "Gavin won't care. And just think of this: You'll be the hit of school. Stinkface is officially losing her title!"

"I'm not sure about that. I just can't believe she's not going."

"Maybe because he dumped her . . . like in Lake Michigan!"

"I have to tell you . . . Eddie said he heard Stinkface and Gavin arguing after first bell," I gossiped.

"About what?" she asked eagerly.

"Eddie said Gavin told Stinkface, 'I can't take your shouting and your magazine mentality.'"

"Bravo! Brilliant, Gavin!" she declared, applauding, but then changed her tone. "And when were you going to tell me this?"

"I was bursting. Truly. But I didn't want to jinx his single status until I knew it for fact."

"I can't believe you!"

"It's just a fluke he asked me at all. It doesn't mean anything—"

"It means you are going to the concert. That means everything!"

I smiled a wild grin.

Jazzy waved her finger at me. "No more secrets!"

"Or sign-ups!" I waved back.

"Agreed. We'll be totally hipster popular now!" Jazzy said, dancing while I modeled a weathered black dress, a silk scarf around my head.

"But I still don't have anything to wear—I look like my grandma in this."

"I might have something. . . ."

"You're twice as tall as me—I'd have to wear stilts! Oh, why did Sid have to be a boy?"

We gazed at the hopeless options strewn on my bed.

"I think this is a job for MasterCard!" said Jazzy.

"Sergeant will kill me. I can only use mine in case of an emergency, Jazz."

"Trix, you're going out with your one dreamboat guy. You've waited all through puberty for this moment. It's like your wedding day and you're going to show up at the altar without a wedding dress. I can think of no bigger emergency than that! We'll go to Groovy Garments. They're the fashion industry's answer to nine-one-one."

Every time Gavin and I passed in the hall, he smiled his usual smile, but he didn't stop to chat and said nothing about the concert. At home, my heart raced every time the phone rang. I checked the messages on the answering machine over and over. I would have called Gavin myself, but each time I picked up the phone, my pulse skyrocketed and my hands began to shake so badly, I couldn't press the numbers.

Finally Wednesday night Sarge told me I had a male caller.

I picked up the phone and said breathlessly, "This is Trixie!"

"This is Ben, from Chaplin's."

"Oh . . . you. I mean, hi!" I added, attempting a perky voice.

"I have a prime opportunity for you. We're having our Amateur Comedy Contest tomorrow."

"I know—Joyce told me. But I won't be able to watch."

"You'll be able to perform."

"Huh?" I asked, distracted. My mind was still on Gavin.

"We had a cancellation. So I signed you up!"

"Signed me up for what?"

"Are you listening? I put you down for the contest!"

Now I was listening. "You did what?" Talent Night Part II flashed before my eyes.

"It'll be great exposure."

I was stunned. First, that Ben expected me to perform the very next night, after it had taken me seventeen years to get the courage to do it once. And second, because tomorrow marked the most important event of my life!

"Just perform the same material from Open Mike."

"I can't!"

"You'll do fine."

"Maybe next time—"

"Next time! Are you crazy? We don't do this every week! The booker will be there. I had to fight to get you a slot! Do you know how many new comics are dying to perform?"

"A billion?"

"Well, less than a billion. But more than five. Seriously, Trixie, you have to do this!"

"Ben—"

"Be here tomorrow at eight thirty. You go on at eight forty-five."

"Eight thirty?" The Varicose Veins concert started at eight.

"You only have to do five minutes. You'll be great!" he said, and hung up.

The phone rang again almost immediately.

"Ben, thanks, but I have other plans!" I confessed.

"Who's Ben?" a somewhat familiar voice asked.

My heart stood still. I couldn't say anything—I was frozen. I was on the phone with Gavin Baldwin! I looked to heaven and mouthed the words, "Thank you!"

"It's Gavin."

"Oh . . . from the hallway!" I blurted out. "I meet so many guys in the hallway, it's hard to keep them all straight."

"Like Ben?"

"Ben? Oh . . . Ben. He's like a brother. A really un-attractive brother!"

"Funny onstage and off," he said in a flirtatious voice. "So we're still on for tomorrow?"

What could I say? "I've waited all my life for a date

with you, but I have a few jokes to tell to some drunk strangers . . . so, thanks, but no." Instead I said, "Sure. Of course!"

"Good. I'll pick you up at seven thirty," he said, and hung up.

I kissed the phone, then ran to my mirror and modeled the pale blue slinky dress I'd bought at Groovy Garments. I gazed at my reflection, wondering how I was going to get out of the most wonderful mess of my life.

At least I had an outfit.

"Ricky and I found this place one day when I couldn't wait until after school for some lip action," Jazzy said, leading me down the deserted stairs by the auditorium stage during lunch. "It's the props room."

"Wow! This is where Sid said he took cigarette breaks. I bet it still smells like smoke."

"I never had to use this before." Jazzy giggled. She switched on a single bare bulb that illuminated a small windowless room full of dust-covered memories from years past: broken Tiffany lamps, yellowed newspapers, beat-up couches, chipped oil paintings, sections of cardboard scenery, a plastic lamppost.

"This is more sticky than the thornbushes of freshman year!" I said, plunking myself down in the middle of a cracked vinyl couch, creating a dust storm.

"If you're going to be the damsel in distress, at least look the part," Jazzy said, tossing me a red feather boa. She grabbed a pipe and detective's hat from a broken trunk for herself and sat in an executive's chair with her feet up on a desk. She rested her head on a backdrop of a senior artist's rendition of the New York skyline.

"You've got to help me, Jazz," I said theatrically, twirling the feather boa. "I don't know what to do! Ha . . . choo! I could call Ben back and say I'm sick," I suggested, searching for a tissue in my purse. "Which I will be if I breathe in this dust much longer."

"The show must go on, darling," Jazzy said with a puff on her pipe. "Besides, this is a golden opportunity. All you've talked and dreamed about is comedy, and now Ben is inviting you to perform at Chaplin's! You might not get a chance to do this ever again!"

"I may never get another chance with Gavin either!" I pointed out, wrapping the boa around my neck.

"Trix, you're not telling him no, either. 'Cause I don't want to hear that you missed your one chance at true lust. Just tell Gavin you have to perform in a contest and you'll be late. But tell him you'll make it up to him when the concert is over!" Jazzy said with a wicked grin.

"You are so in the gutter!"

"All right. Let me think," she pondered, tipping her hat over her eyes. "What time do the Veins start?"

"Eight."

"And what time is Chaplin's contest?"

"Eight."

"But when exactly do you have to perform?"

"Eight forty-five, but I have to be there—"

"By George, I think I've got it!" she exclaimed, jumping to her feet and knocking over Manhattan. "Chaplin's is around the corner from the Mosh Pit. There's your answer. You can totally do both! You hang with Gavin until eight thirty, tell him you have to go to the bathroom, run to Chaplin's for your gig and then hop back to the Mosh Pit and dance the night away!"

"That's crazy!"

"Darling, it's brilliant!"

"I can't do it!"

"You must," she insisted.

"It's impossible."

"Difficult, yes, but not impossible. Most girls spend half an hour in the bathroom. He'll never know you're gone!"

"But I won't have time to prepare for the contest. I have to sign in, take twenty deep breaths, rehearse my material in the bathroom, drink a Coke, bite my nails. I have a whole routine. And then when I'm back with Gavin, I'll be disheveled and exhausted. I won't have the strength to dance. He'll never smile at me again!"

"Are you going to sit at home and watch Jelly Bean till you're an old woman? You have to grab life by the horns!"

I caressed the feather boa. "Can I grab life by the horns and watch TV?"

SMILEY-FACE WATCH

Thursday morning I begged Dad to take Sarge to Maggiano's that night for spaghetti so I could have total privacy for my dream date. He obliged and I slipped him a copy of *Golf Digest* and a kiss on the cheek as they exited for the evening. Even Sid had called me to prep me for my date: "Don't be nervous," he said. "Just pretend I'm with you."

I was finally going on my sizzling dream date—this was one time I didn't want to pretend my big brother was sitting right next to me.

I obsessively retouched my coffee-colored lipstick and smoothed out my silky Groovy Garments dress in the hallway mirror. I had dreamed of this day for two long years—Gavin showing up at my house with roses; Gavin bringing me chicken soup when I was home with the flu; Gavin picking me up for the prom; Gavin begging me to elope with him to Las Vegas. But here I was, waiting for him to take me to a Varicose Veins concert in Amber Hills.

I fingered the most important part of my ensemble for the evening—my smiley-face watch—and stared into the hallway mirror.

I anxiously sat in the audience of the ornate theater, wringing my hands. A suntanned, tuxedoed movie-star presenter twinkled from behind the glass podium. "And now the award for Best Girlfriend of Gavin Baldwin—," he said, opening the elegant envelope. "And the Valentine goes to Trixie Shapiro!"

I was overwhelmed as I rose from my seat. I felt faint walking precariously up the white-marble stairs to the stage. I stood next to the presenter in my strapless glittering silver gown. Tears of joy streamed down my face.

"I wasn't sure I'd win, so I didn't prepare a speech—but my mother did!" I pulled a note from my dress that unscrolled to the floor. The audience roared.

"I'd like to thank my agent, Cupid, my clothes designer, Jazlyn Peters, and my real-life producers, Mom and Dad." I lifted up the diamond Valentine. "And a special thanks to Gavin Baldwin, for always being in the hallway, and for making this night possible!"

The doorbell rang. I nearly jumped out of my dress. I dashed to the door and peeked through the peephole. Gavin Baldwin was distorted, his head bloated, but still gorgeous, and calm—not like me, who stood melting and shaking all at once.

He rang the bell again.

I opened the door to the whole Gavin—sexy in his black-leather coat, a flashing stud earring, brand-new denim jeans, and black boots. His blue eyes glistened, his jet-black hair shined, his smile sparkled bigger than a July Fourth celebration.

Parked on the curb was the familiar Volvo. Now I was going to see my favorite car, but from the inside. I bit my lip. This was my James Dean, my Elvis, my favorite Beatle. I didn't want to blow it. So I said nothing as we walked to his car.

"I'm surprised I didn't have to meet your parents," he said, opening the passenger door for me. "Don't you watch talk shows? You can't be too careful dating these days," he said protectively.

"Don't you watch talk shows? You can't be too careful having parents either!"

Gavin laughed.

I melted into the leather seat and caressed its smooth surface with my hands. How many times had Stinkface sat in this very same place? Did she appreciate his love-mobile as much as I? Or was she the kind of girl to put her feet up on the dashboard, smoke cigarettes, and roll down the window when the air-conditioning was on?

Why should I care? Stinkface was somewhere else right now, and I had the best seat in the house—or rather, car.

I flipped down the visor and looked in the mirror to prove to myself that I was really sitting in Gavin Baldwin's Volvo. I smoothed my lips together, and he caught me out of the corner of his eyes. I was embarrassing myself already and I'd only been with him for two minutes.

I quickly flipped up the visor. "It's a new flavor from Nifty lipstick," I confessed flippantly. "It's called Luscious Latte."

"Cheaper than an espresso—"

"And half the fat!"

We both laughed. Then there was a long silence as he fiddled with the radio and I adjusted my dress.

"Have you ever seen the Veins before?" Gavin finally asked.

"Does cable count?"

"I guess."

"Then yes. My seats were amazing!"

"They are actually taller than twenty-five inches in person."

I laughed.

"Finally I get a reaction from you. I was beginning to think you didn't laugh at other people's jokes."

We passed Chaplin's on the way to the Mosh Pit. The

club's sign seemed to shout: "Trixie Shapiro! Don't forget about me!"

"You go to Chaplin's a lot?" he asked, also noticing the sign.

"Does tonight count?" I wanted to confess. "More than I care to admit," I answered instead.

My watch smiled 7:45 as we stepped out of the parking lot. But a more watchful clock ticked loudly inside my head.

My plan was to tell Gavin at 8:35 that I was going to the bathroom. I calculated I would be gone fifteen minutes, which included running to Chaplin's, performing, and running back. Upon my return, I'd say, "You should have seen the line!"

Gavin held both tickets as we entered the Mosh Pit, confirming our status as an official couple. I yearned to bump into some trendy gossip queen, but we didn't see anyone from Mason as we pressed through the crowd.

By 8:20 we were dancing to the beat of the Varicose Veins, and several times Gavin even pulsed his body right up against mine. I tingled all over, but became distracted at the sight of my watch. It was suddenly 8:36.

"I have to go to the bathroom."

But Gavin continued to dance.

"I've got to go to the bathroom!" I shouted.

"I can't hear you!"

He stopped dancing and leaned in close. As I fell asleep each night, I had fantasized whispering millions of things into Gavin's ear, but "I have to go to the bathroom" was not one of them.

"I'll go with you," he said.

This was definitely not part of the plan. What would Jazzy do now?

"No, really. It'll only take a minute."

"You shouldn't go alone."

"I've been going to the bathroom alone for years!"

If there was ever a moment a girl didn't need Mr. Sensitive, this was it. Why couldn't Gavin be more like Eddie? Eddie wouldn't have cared if I left with a motorcycle gang I met while waiting in line for a bratwurst.

"Let's go," he said firmly.

On any other day I would have fainted away at the notion that Gavin Baldwin insisted on going with me to the girls' room.

"I can go alone. I have to go alone! It makes me nervous . . . I mean . . ."

He firmly grabbed my hand and led me toward the rest rooms.

He was holding my hand. It was the most perfect hand in the world. But this was getting totally out of control, I thought, as we squeezed through the crowd, looking for the rest rooms. The first time Gavin holds my hand and I want him to let go.

The women's room loomed ahead. What was I doing? I was leaving this sexy superdude to stand before a crowd of drunken strangers.

"I'll wait by the T-shirt stand," he said.

I opened the rest room door and looked at my terrified face in the mirror. I took a deep breath and then peeked my head out the door. Through the crowd I saw Gavin holding up a Varicose Veins T-shirt to the salesperson.

I crept out behind two wide bodies. Then I bolted toward the exit sign.

I ran to Chaplin's, cursing my fashion pride as my toes smashed against my high-heeled boots. Next time I get in a mess like this, I wear sneakers.

I arrived at the club panting.

"Where have you been?" Ben asked at the door.

I tried to catch my breath.

"Never mind! I'll sign you in. You almost lost your slot! But it's your lucky night, girl. We're running fifteen minutes behind," he informed me, heading toward the judges' table.

Fifteen minutes? I checked my watch. It was already 8:50.

I didn't know whether the other comics lacked talent or if it was my own anxiety that made their jokes as stale as three-year-old bubble gum. After all, I could have still been dancing with my dream angel, happily wondering if he would kiss me. But instead I was sitting alone in a smoky club, listening to a pilot talk on and on about flying. Where were the punch lines? Had he left them in the cockpit?

Weeks ago I might have been sympathetic to this man, standing up and making a fool of himself. But all I could think now was, why isn't he being cleared for takeoff? Why is he wasting his time? Why is he wasting my time?

My watch was ticking louder and louder, the smiley face staring back at me cheerfully.

A college-age guy wearing a Giants cap, a white Miller Lite T-shirt, and torn blue jeans sat down beside me. "Are you performing, little lady?"

Normally I would have been put off by such a remark and responded with a sarcastic comment. But instead I made an exception and answered his question.

"So how old are you?" he asked.

"Forty-four," I replied.

"Well, you don't look a day over sixteen," he said with a wink. "Can I get you something?"

"Are you a waiter?" I asked.

"At one time or another we're all waiters."

I should have asked him a million questions, but I was too distracted to think clearly. I could see Gavin trying to look into the women's bathroom—or dancing with a supermodel.

Smooth Operator returned, setting down a beer and a Coke, straws poking out of each drink. "Here you go, little lady. I'm Cam."

"Trixie," I responded. "So, this isn't your first time, I take it?" I asked, taking a sip from the straw.

"Do you always ask that to strange comics who buy you drinks?"

"Do you always sip beer through a straw?"

"I may look rugged on the outside, little lady, but on the inside I'm as meek as a lamb. I'm not in the contest. I'm featuring this week. They're giving me time tonight so I can get a feel for the room."

"I thought you looked familiar."

"You're one of my five fans, eh?" he asked, cozying up to me.

"I saw the poster in the lobby."

"Oh," he said dejectedly. "Tell me, where's a good place to unwind in this town after the show?"

Normally I would have been flattered to be chatting with a professional comedian about Chicago's nightlife, but tonight I had to get back to the Mosh Pit.

A honky-tonk comic with an acoustic guitar bounced off the tiny stage.

"You're next," Ben called, waving to me from

behind the judges' table.

"Now we have a funny girl, the only female performing tonight and more importantly, the only performer young enough to need a fake ID. Let's welcome to the stage . . . Trixie Shapiro!"

I heard my name and the courteous applause. I ran to the stage and grabbed the microphone.

"I just came from the Mosh Pit, where the Varicose Veins are in concert," I began breathlessly. "My mother doesn't understand why I'd pay to see them. I told her that when her varicose veins can play guitar, I'll pay to see them too!"

The audience laughed, and I felt the rush of their energy. For the next five minutes I forgot about the Mosh Pit, a guy named Gavin, and the smiley-face watch.

Then the flashing light signaled my time was up.

"Well, I gotta go. I have to be in bed by ten!"

My body felt electric as I stepped offstage. Audience members smiled at me and said, "You were great!" as I passed. Ben gave me a huge hug.

"See, there was nothing to be nervous about, girl. I knew you could do it. The judges loved your impression of the first lady, and I loved the Varicose Veins bit. Topical stuff is always a winner!"

The Varicose Veins? I had totally forgotten. It was 9:20!

"See you later, Ben."

"But you can't go. They're giving out the prize tonight."

Prize? My prize was waiting for me at the Mosh Pit, if someone else hadn't claimed him by now.

"Stay here. I'll be right back," Ben said.

I quickly grabbed my purse.

"Great job, little lady, not that I'm surprised," Cam said, sitting down at my table.

"It was great meeting you," I said quickly.

"You're not leaving! You have to stay and watch my set. I go on next."

I was torn. What should I do? The man of my dreams was patiently waiting for me by the T-shirt stand. But if I left now, I would miss an opportunity to befriend a professional comedian.

I reluctantly set my purse back down.

Cam ran onstage and took my mind off the Mosh Pit. He was far superior to the amateurs. Naturally his material was better, but he was also poised, polished, and in total command of his audience.

"You were fabulous!" I said when he returned to the table. "But I've got to run."

He shot me a look of surprise, then disappointment.

"That's right. That thing about being in bed by ten. Come back if you get a chance; I'm here all week," he said with lonely eyes.

★ ★ ★

The Windy City was blowing against me as I flew back to the Mosh Pit. At the first corner I had to hold on to a stop sign for support. The Varicose Veins ticket stub flew out of my hands and blew down the sidewalk.

"Oh, no," I cried, running after the stub. Just as I bent down, the wind picked it up again and carried it into the busy street.

"Help!" I screamed, as if someone had stolen my purse. I ran into the street after it. A cab swerved around me, blaring its horn.

I ran in hot pursuit of the most important ticket of my life. The stub finally came to rest underneath a parked car. Exhausted, I tried to reach it from the street, but my arm didn't stretch far enough.

Then I noticed a spike-haired punk with more tattoos than skin, eyeing me. He knew it was worth something. I quickly ran to the curb as he reached under the car and grabbed the stub.

"Wow! The Varicose Veins," the tattooed menace said. "It's sold out!"

"I know. Give it back."

"I bet this cost you something, pretty girl."

"Give it to me now."

"If you think they're so great, why'd you leave the concert?"

"It's none of your business. Give me back my ticket or I'm calling the cops!" Then I mumbled, "Or my mother—which will be a lot worse."

"How much is this ticket worth to ya?" he asked, fingering the stub.

The ticket was worth everything. My clothes, my watch, my purse. My money. But if I offered him my accessories, there was no guarantee he'd give me the ticket.

I was so high on adrenaline, I was ready to kill.

He caressed the ticket as I caressed my mace. I had never used it, but Sergeant made me keep it on my key chain. Did it work? Maybe it had expired. Did mace expire? I couldn't check now.

I had taken self-defense classes long ago, but never offense classes. The only fighting I had ever done was with Sid, and he always won. I saw myself lying tattered and shoeless in the gutter while the Tattooed Menace partied at the Mosh Pit, sharing beers with Gavin, slinky babes on either side of them.

"You're right," I said abruptly. "The Veins suck! They're great on CD, but at the Mosh Pit they're rancid. I guess it's the acoustics—and the fact that the singer has laryngitis. Have a good time! I'm going home." I walked away.

The Tattooed Menace stood speechless. His Golden Ticket was suddenly worthless.

"Next time you should see Aerosmith!" he called to

me. "They always rock!" He tore the stub in two, lit a cigarette, and walked the other way.

I breathlessly presented the torn stub to the gnarly doorman.

"Man, someone hated this concert! Did you find this in the street?"

"No. It's mine."

"Where'd you get this?" the gothic gargoyle asked.

"I bought it."

"A scalper sold you a torn ticket stub?"

"No, I bought the ticket. Actually my date bought them. And he's in there right now waiting for me." Or so I hoped.

"Must be some date if you left without him," he said flirtatiously. "We don't honor torn ticket stubs. But you can sit here with me."

"You have to let me in—he's my ride home."

"I can call a cab. Or better yet, I can take you home myself."

"Bob, I need your counter," a man said from inside the club.

The gothic gargoyle sauntered into the coat checkroom. I eyed the red rope. I'd never snuck in anywhere before, but was it really sneaking in if I had a ticket—torn or not?

I hopped over the rope and made a dash for the dance floor.

I had made it back—alive. My heart started racing again. Would Gavin still be here? Would I find him with a gorgeous blonde? How would I explain spending over an hour in the bathroom? I wished I was back onstage in front of strangers.

I didn't see Gavin anywhere. He wasn't on the dance floor, and he wasn't by the phones or the T-shirt booth. He wasn't at the beer stand. He wasn't near the bathrooms. He wasn't by the coat check. He was gone.

I'd blown everything. I'd lost my only chance at my dream man. Why had I gone to Chaplin's? I couldn't blame Gavin for going home.

I leaned on the balcony overlooking the dance floor. I might as well hear some of the Veins. At least I could tell Jazzy what songs they played.

I stared out onto the stage, four skinny musicians jamming, highlighted by red neon and slithering fog. The crowd singing, dancing, tightly squeezed together, a sea of black clothes amid overflowing smoke and fog. Everyone looked the same.

But one person glowed in the dark on the dance floor below—Gavin! He seemed distracted, like he was looking for someone.

I didn't know what I would say, but I didn't care. I ran

down to the dance floor and pushed through the crowd. "Gavin! Gavin!"

I finally reached him and hugged him hard.

"Gavin, I couldn't find you!"

Like a father who has lost his child at the playground and then finds her, Gavin went through several emotions, anger being the first.

"Where have you been?" he yelled. "I waited forever for you. After several eons I thought maybe you had come out of the bathroom, so I came back here to the dance floor. But the fog machine poured out so much smoke, I couldn't see anything. So I went back to the concessions, thinking maybe you were waiting for me by the T-shirt booth. I checked the phones, the parking lot. I was just going to call your house!"

"I'm sorry. I guess we kept missing each other."

"I bet it's against code to have all this fog going when the club's filled to capacity," he said, calming down.

I gave him a wry smile.

"It looks like you've been through hell too," he joked, placing my dress strap back on my shoulder.

"Yes, I'm totally frazzled."

"I never should have gone to the souvenir stand. But now we've found each other," he said, pulling me close.

I melted against him in a long embrace.

"Wanna dance?" he finally asked.

We bopped to the fast pulse of the bass. I threw my whole body into the mix, swaying, rocking my hips, and stretching my arms overhead as if we were alone in my room and I was dancing just for him.

"I'm clapping for you," he said after the song was over. I melted.

We danced closely through all three encores.

He held my hand as the lights came on. "The T-shirts are awesome. I should know—I stared at them for about an hour. Want one?"

I hated concert T-shirts. They were always too big and extremely overpriced, but a shirt was a souvenir of our night together, and I wanted all the proof I could get. I'd pay anything.

Instead Gavin paid—a black Veins shirt for him and a red one for me.

"You look great in red," Gavin said as I held it against myself. We walked out, hand in hand, T-shirts dangling from our free hands.

Gavin stopped talking when we reached his car.

"Something wrong?" I asked, leaning against the passenger door. "Did you lose your keys?"

"I've had a taste for coffee all night," he said, his keys now jingling in his hand.

"There's a coffee shop on the corner."

"I'm not talking about Starbucks," he said. Then he leaned over and kissed my mocha-flavored lips.

He kissed me long and leaned his body up against mine. I thought I was going to explode.

"Much better than Starbucks," he said as we got in the car.

Gavin's words gave me a more powerful jolt than drinking ten caffe lattes with double espresso!

ARE YOU TALKING TO ME?

☆

I was helping Sergeant load the dishwasher after dinner the next night when the phone rang.

"It's a young man," Sergeant said loudly, handing me the receiver.

"Sshhh! He'll hear you!" I yelled, embarrassed.

"He didn't hear me."

"Believe me, everyone hears you!" I shouted, running up the stairs. "I'll get it in my room."

I plopped on my fluffy bed.

"Thirsty for some more coffee?" I said flirtatiously.

"Coffee?" another guy's voice said. My stomach dropped in embarrassment.

It was Ben. "Where the hell did you go last night?"

"I told you I couldn't perform—"

"It doesn't matter. . . . I just called to tell you that you friggin' won!"

The words echoed in my head. "Won what?"

"The Amateur Comedy Contest. You won!"

"The contest or a door prize?"

"Do I have the wrong Trixie Shapiro?"

"I won?"

"Yes. You won."

"I can't believe it! This is so unreal. Are you sure?"

"It was between you and the pilot. Yes, I'm sure."

"Ben, this is unbelievable!"

"Congrats!"

"I never win anything. Not even a free Sprite when I open a can of pop." I was stunned. "Can I tell my friends?"

"You can tell the world."

"Not that I have many friends to tell. By the way, what did I win?"

"That's what I've been trying to tell you! You won a digital video camera."

"A video camera? No way! A video camera?"

"Trix, I can't talk—"

"Do you know what I can do with a video camera? I can tape everything! Me and Jazz at the mall, me and my talk shows . . . My—"

"Your act?"

"I really have an act now, don't I?"

"Listen, I can't talk. I was just getting you on the phone for the booker. Hang on a sec, but don't ramble. Okay?"

"Ben? Ben? Ben? Are you there?" Maybe this was a

joke—Ben's way of getting me back for coming late and leaving early. "Ben, this isn't funny!"

"I'll be the judge of what's funny," another man's voice said. "I'm Vic. I book the comedians at Chaplin's. Where did you run off to last night?"

"I had . . . another show," I said truthfully.

"Well, your act was great—great material. This business is short on females. And with the high school angle, you've got yourself a hook. And you look comfortable, you just need more stage time. Your impression of the first lady was perfect!"

"Thanks," I replied, stunned.

"I need an emcee next week."

"Emcee? Me?"

"I have the headliner and feature acts. I just need an opener. Are you there?"

"Am I where?"

"Use the same material you performed last night, mention our sponsor, and introduce the comedians. Wednesday through Sunday."

I didn't even hear the dates. He wants me to emcee? To be part of the actual show? Winning an amateur contest was enough—I'd take the video camera and call it a day. I should quit while I'm ahead. Although I had fantasized about this all my life, the reality was difficult to grasp.

"We'll start you out at two hundred."

Two hundred dollars? Did I hear him right? Maybe he said two dollars.

I scrambled for a pen, but I couldn't find a piece of paper. All I had was the Varicose Veins ticket stubs. I scribbled the dates, times, and names of the comedians—Tucker Jones and Cam—on my tiny love souvenir.

I placed the phone on my nightstand and started screaming.

"Are you all right?" Sergeant shouted, bursting into my room.

She found me jumping up and down on my bed, kissing the ticket stubs.

"I thought you were hurt! You almost gave me a heart attack!"

"You'll never believe what happened!"

"You dusted your shelves?"

"No, this is way bigger. Bigger than a sparkling kitchen floor!"

"I'm waiting. . . ."

"I won a comedy contest—and now they want me to perform in a real show! I'll have a real microphone and a real audience! And a video camera and two hundred smiling George Washingtons to prove it."

"A contest? At school? Congratulations!"

"No, at Chaplin's!"

"Chaplin's?" she asked, suddenly changing her tone. "I let you visit Chaplin's to get you away from the TV and out of the house. But to watch—not to perform. Besides, I thought you gave up that dream."

"Ben signed me up. It's a fluke I got a spot in the show at all!"

"I don't understand. You didn't even tell me you entered. Don't you have to have parental permission?"

"It was a contest, not a field trip!"

"But your father and I would love to have seen you!"

"It was a last-minute thing, Ma, otherwise—"

"Trixie, you should be spending your evenings studying. Chaplin's isn't a place for a teenage girl. And all that cigarette smoke—it's not a healthy environment."

"It's no worse than Sid's dorm. I get secondhand smoke just talking to him on the phone."

"Sid's in college, but you still live under my roof."

"A lot of kids have jobs after school."

"But not until midnight! Besides, I don't want you to endure another Talent Night. It was hard on you."

"I don't either—so make sure you're not in the audience."

"You don't want us to come?"

"I'll videotape the show. Then you can watch it over and over, while you're vacuuming."

"You're being paid?" she inquired slowly.

"Yes! Can you believe it?"

"You really won?"

"I really won!"

"It's not what I envisioned for you . . . but you won!"

I smiled a wild grin.

"But . . . one week," she warned. "Not one day more! No drinking, no smoking, no passive dating. And if anyone heckles you, you tell the owner, the cops, or better yet—me."

"Of course!"

"Congratulations!" she said with a huge hug.

"Thanks, Ma," I exclaimed, kissing her on the cheek.

"But one week and then you trade your comedy notebook in for your English notebook," she said, leaving.

"Deal," I called through the door.

"Our baby won a comedy contest!" I heard Sarge yell to my dad, as she ran down the stairs.

FEATURING

☆ ☆ ☆

STARBABY

☆

S tuck-up *Melrose Place* wannabes who didn't know I was alive two weeks ago now stared at me as I walked through the halls. Not because I was going to be a real comedian at Chaplin's for a week, but because I was on the arm of Gavin Baldwin. I felt like the first lady, although no one asked for my autograph—yet.

Our relationship consisted of phone calls, school lunches, and our first movie together.

We had just a few days before my gig at Chaplin's. The time I didn't spend rehearsing and writing in my comedy journal, I devoted to Gavin.

One day at lunch I found Gavin sitting against a tree by the baseball field, writing in a notebook.

"Finishing your homework for fifth bell?" I asked, leaning over him.

"Uh, no," he said, pulling the notebook to his chest.

"Is it a love poem?" I asked coyly.

"Whatever!" he said, covering the words from my sight.

I grabbed the notebook and ran around the other side of the tree.

"Don't, Trixie—," he moaned, rising.

I began to read an eloquently written narrative about a father and son at a baseball game. "This is great, Gavin! Is the boy you?"

"Give it back," he warned, stepping closer.

I stepped back and continued to read, but he caught me, tickling my belly until I released the notebook from my grasp.

"Is this for class?" I asked, following him back.

"No—I just jot down my thoughts, like you jot down jokes."

"You can write! You should submit it to the *Mason Mag.*"

"It's crap," he said. He ripped the page from the notebook, crumbled it up, and threw it over the school fence.

"What are you doing?" I asked. "You could be the next F. Scott Fitzgerald."

"I'll be more like the next W. Robert Baldwin, my father. Apparently Baldwins are more practical than you theatrical dream–chasing Shapiros," he teased, poking me in the side. "I'm going to be an architect, just like my dad."

"Really?" I asked, impressed. I was pleased Gavin was sharing his dreams with me. Or were they his dreams?

"But is that what you want to do?"

"Does it matter?" he asked. "Let's quit talking," he said, and kissed me long, taking my mind off anything but his lips.

I made greeting cards with silly poems, hung candy on his locker, and brought him cupcakes for lunch.

One afternoon we were sitting on Mason's back steps. He was reading a note I'd written to him during first bell—a sprinkle-filled note with heart stickers surrounding a cartoonish drawing of him that read: "World's Hottest Hipster."

"So why do you like me?" I asked. "Is it because of the stickers? Or the sprinkles?"

He shook his head at me and looked away.

"Because I leave cute phone messages on your voice mail? Because you want to be an architect and I buy you Frank Lloyd Wright cards? And leave stuffed animals in your locker?"

He folded the note and put it in his pocket.

"Really, tell me why," I begged.

"Because there's more to you than a pretty face, Starbaby."

"There is?" I leaned against Gavin's shoulder and whispered my new name—Starbaby Shapiro!

"Hi, honey, I'm home," Gavin said, entering the heart-shaped mansion he had designed especially for us. "I missed you all day, sweetie!" He kissed me with love-filled lips. "I'll pick you up from Chaplin's when you're finished tonight. I know you don't like me to watch you perform."

"But you don't have to show up in the limo with roses—"

"Tonight I'll do more. I've bought Chaplin's for you, and I'm calling it Trixie's!"

"I can't wait to see you perform soon," Gavin said, bringing me back to reality.

"But you can't!" I exclaimed.

"Of course I can. You'll need a cameraman to videotape you. And you'll need a bodyguard to protect you from all your new fans."

"You mean hecklers! No, you can't come, really."

"I've seen you perform already, remember?"

"But I didn't know you were there!"

"I'll be as quiet as a librarian."

Gavin at Chaplin's? Sitting in the front row? His gorgeous baby-blue eyes watching me as I drew a comic blank? What if I didn't live up to his expectations? What if I bombed?

The bell rang.

"See you later, Starbaby," he said, kissing me on the cheek and hurrying away to class.

Starbaby!

I glowed from the sound of my new nickname—a vast improvement on "Shrimp."

DIVA DOCUMENTARY

☆

"Make love to the camera!" Jazzy instructed, squinting through the video camera on the southbound el. "Next stop the *Douglas Douglas Show!*" she yelled to bewildered travelers. "Trix, you'll be a household name. We can share a mansion in L.A. with gardeners and personal trainers and have facials and body massages anytime we want. And our very own houseboy!"

"What about Ricky?" I asked, looking into the camera.

"He can live in the guesthouse," Jazzy said. "I don't want him getting in the way of the action."

I hid my face behind *Teen People*, embarrassed by the sudden attention.

"You know, the famous are often very shy. It may take me days to reveal her real personality," Jazzy said to a shopaholic grandmother sitting across from us.

"Who is she?" the woman inquired, clutching her Neiman Marcus bag.

"Trixie Shapiro—Teenage Comedienne!"

I pulled down my hat in disgust. "I'm not famous," I mumbled.

"Can I have your autograph?" the woman asked eagerly.

I felt guilty as I signed her copy of the *Tribune*.

After a trip to the Water Tower shops, Jazzy and I took a cab to Navy Pier and sat on a bench, bundled up in our L.L. Bean coats. "Ricky and I are coming to watch you this Saturday," Jazzy confessed.

"I told you not to come," I replied.

"But I discovered you!"

"And look what happened on Talent Night."

"Forget about that. You'll be styling!"

"I can't risk it. I'm doing this for more than a grade now, Jazz—they're paying me."

"Okay, I won't come this week. But you have to let me come next time."

"There won't be a next time."

"Don't be so grim. You'll be performing on Broadway soon, and I'm going to get tired of watching the video."

"Me on Broadway?" I said sarcastically. "If that happens, you can sit onstage."

"So what's it really like to perform?" Jazzy asked a few minutes later. She was filming me in front of the pier's massive Ferris wheel.

"You know. You've performed."

"I was onstage for two minutes. And I spent most of that time trying to get out from under my cardboard Romeo. Besides, this is your documentary, not mine. So shut up and talk!"

I gazed up at the Ferris wheel.

"Is it like sex?" Jazzy hinted.

"How should I know?"

"Oh yeah, I forgot. Is it like getting wasted?"

I glared at her through the lens.

"Is it like being thrown into a bush by a gang of testosterone-driven seniors?"

"Sometimes!"

"Is it like flipping through *Cosmo* and stuffing your face with Twizzlers?"

"No! No! No! It's the biggest rush!" I declared as Jazzy zoomed in. "It's like being electrified. For those five minutes I'm not alone. I belong, I have a purpose. I connect—I don't worry about anything—my future, my past, anything. I feel euphoric."

"And if they don't laugh?"

"I'll stay in bed and hide under the covers!"

"That's a wrap," Jazzy shouted, turning off the camera. "I don't care what you say. It sounds like sex to me." We giggled as we gathered our belongings and headed for the train.

LIVE FROM CHAPLIN'S

☆

Wednesday night I began my gig at Chaplin's. The show started at 8:30 with a second show on Friday and Saturday.

"Break a leg, sweetheart," my dad said, giving me a kiss on the cheek when he pulled into Chaplin's parking lot. "Are you sure you don't want me to stay?"

"Dad, I'm freaking as it is! You'll be with me here," I said, pointing to my heart.

I plunked myself down at my home away from home—a little table at the back of the club.

"Last time you were late—now you're early," Ben remarked.

"I was afraid there might be traffic."

"You live two blocks away!"

"There could have been a parade for all I knew," I said, biting my fingernails.

"Can I get you a pop?" he offered.

"I'll be running to the bathroom every two minutes."

"Then I'll leave you to veg out or Zen out or

whatever you do."

"Freak out. That's what I do!"

I had brought my comedy notebook to review my material. For diversion I'd also brought a Walkman with a Celestial Seas tape and a stack of magazines. But they failed to distract me. All too soon the audience would be filling the empty tables and expecting nonstop laughs. And I was supposed to remain calm and read about abstinence in *Seventeen*? Instead I fervently stared at my comedy notebook and bit my nails.

"Does performing get any easier?" I asked Ben when he came back to check on me.

"How should I know? I just—"

"Maybe I need a straitjacket to calm me down. Or an injection of Valium."

"Maybe you need some more nails," he said.

"Tell me again what I do tonight," I said nervously.

"You have to announce Cam, the feature, and Tucker Jones, the headliner. When they arrive, ask them how they want to be introduced. At the end of the show thank our sponsor, the Amber Hills Hotel, remind the audience to fill out the comment card on the table, and announce that Martin Evans and Eli Rosenthal are appearing next week. Mention that Eli's been on Showtime."

"I'll be lucky if I remember my own name," I said, horrified.

The club was starting to fill up when a guy in a base-ball cap walked up to me.

"I didn't think I'd ever see you again," Cam said, sur-prised.

"I'm hosting the show. Can you believe it? I won the contest!"

"Next week I'll be opening for you," he said. "Nervous?"

"You kidding? I do this all the time. Just like plucking my eyebrows."

"Remember you have the microphone, not them," he comforted me.

"Thanks. I'll try to remember that. Oh yeah, how do you want to be introduced?"

"How about 'Voted *People*'s Sexiest Man Alive!'"

I glared at him.

"Okay, how about 'Performed on Comedy Central and opened for Steven Wright'?"

I quickly scribbled the intro on a Chaplin's napkin when a shaggy-haired grunger guy walked in with two buddies.

"That's Tucker." Cam pointed.

I took a breath and approached him like a mouse. "I'm opening the show," I said meekly. "How should I intro-duce you?"

"I've been on the *Douglas Douglas Show.*"

"You have?" I asked in awe.

Ben tapped me on the shoulder. "Ready, girl?"

I looked at Cam as I bit my lip.

"She's ready!" he announced.

My stomach sank to the floor. My heart raced as if I had just finished a marathon. I had a lump in my throat the size of the Sears Tower!

"And here's . . . Trixie Shapiro," Ben announced from offstage.

I walked in slow motion, like I was in a thick soup, trying to keep my noodle legs and carrot arms from floating away. Finally I reached the stage and stepped behind the microphone, which towered over me.

I paused, looked up at the microphone and down at myself. The audience snickered at the height difference. I tilted the microphone stand down to my level and looked out.

"I need a microphone to use the microphone!"

They laughed. Exhilaration surged through my whole being.

I was well into my set, bantering with a group of dentists at the table to my right, when I glimpsed the theater door opening. A delivery boy entered with a pizza. It was Eddie.

I was stunned. Why was he delivering now? Was he

going to stay and watch me?

Eddie didn't even notice me as he handed the pizza to Ben. Then Ben pointed at the stage. I couldn't say anything as Eddie sat down. I glared at Ben, who must have seen me struggling. I could see him trying to shoo Eddie away, but Eddie didn't move.

He looked straight at me and smiled. All I could think of was Eddie watching me. I couldn't remember my next joke.

I wanted to stop the show. "Give me some privacy!" I wanted to scream. I felt like I was in Mason's bathroom stall and Eddie had accidentally opened the door.

I glared back at Eddie, hoping he'd get the hint.

Finally Ben picked up the pizza and grabbed Eddie's arm, and they slipped into the kitchen.

"Hey, we're over here!" a drunken dentist called. "Don't forget about us!"

"Believe me, a shot of Novocain wouldn't save me from your painful heckling!" I improvised. The dentists laughed and my heart beat once again.

After the show I was glowing from my comedy high and relaxing alone at my table when Eddie pulled up a chair and set down a piping hot, small cheeseless pizza with extra sauce.

"You'll have to pick another route," I demanded. "You can't deliver here anymore."

"Get a grip, baby, you totally rocked!"

"We're going over to Hailey's Pub," Cam said to me, approaching the table. "You comin'?"

"No thanks," I answered. "I have plans."

"Your boyfriend?" Cam asked, glancing at Eddie.

"He's just the delivery boy."

"Don't insult me like that," Eddie scolded. "I'm the delivery man!"

I was still flying. Cam, Eddie, and I were buzzing through Chaplin's parking lot when Gavin got out of his Volvo. I was elated to see my dream boy picking me up after my dream job.

"Your dad looks really good in combat boots," Eddie teased me. "You're a little late for the show," he called to Gavin.

"He's right on time!" I said, running over and giving him a squeeze. But Gavin's body was stiff. He didn't kiss me and reluctantly opened my door.

I could feel a chill in the car, and it wasn't from the air-conditioning. "So you let Eddie watch?" Gavin asked accusingly.

"No, he sat in the kitchen. He said the cook was hilarious!"

Gavin gave me an icy look and buckled his seat belt.

"I can prove it. I've got the videotape! Seriously, Gavin. You have to understand. I'm just a beginner. But after Sunday this'll all be over. The only giggling I'll be doing is from your tickling."

"Friday night a bunch of us are going to see the original *Rocky*."

"A bunch?"

"Sam, me, Jenny, and Kitty."

"Jenny and Kitty? That's not a bunch! That's a double date!"

"It would be a double date if you were coming."

"You, Sam, and two cheerleaders?"

"I'm not going to sit home on a Friday night, Trixie."

"Of course, I'm not asking you to. I'll cancel the show. I'll call in sick."

"You can't do that."

"I'll tell them my heart broke," I said, tears filling my eyes.

"Chill out, Starbaby," he said.

I hugged him hard, ashamed of my oozing vulnerability.

Gavin and I sat at my usual table at the back of the club, watching a budding female teenage comic rule the room with her jokes about high school. Everyone in the club was laughing, except me.

*She ended her routine to a Godzilla-sized laugh, replaced
the mike, and smiled a cutesy smile. The audience rose and
applauded wildly. Gavin turned to me and said, "She was
hilarious. That girl's going to be a star!"*

*"Too bad we can't stay to get her autograph," I said, with-
out passion. "I have to get back to my dorm and finish my
thesis on the history of stage fright."*

I stared out the window as we pulled out of the parking lot. This was the first time my fantasy had turned into
a nightmare.

Chaplin's bright neon sign blinked several times
before it finally turned off for the night.

I wasn't ready for my light to be turned off.

"I'm outa here," Cam said to me Sunday night after
his set.

"But Tucker's still performing."

"Yeah, but I've been paid. There aren't curtain calls in
comedy, little lady."

"You can't leave!"

"Miss me already?"

The truth was I did. I had sat with Cam every night
during Tucker's set at my hidden table, and now my
comic mate was going to be on a plane to San
Francisco.

"I'm next door at the lovely Amber Hills Hotel. Room two thirteen," he offered.

I was afraid I'd never see him again, and I was desperate to keep my professional comedy connections. I wanted to find out more about the business, what life was like on the road, how to get booked at other clubs, how to improve my act. But what if I found out more than I wanted to know?

Suddenly I remembered my promise to Sergeant. She had agreed to let Ben drive me home, so I could hang out for my last hurrah. According to my watch, I wouldn't turn into a pumpkin for one more hour.

Vic counted out ten twenty-dollar bills in his back-stage office. "I just need your autograph on the receipt."

I caressed the money.

"And I need an emcee in two weeks. Can I put you down?"

In my hand I held more money than I'd received at my Bat Mitzvah! And I was paid for doing the one thing I loved the most—making people laugh.

But what about the wrath of Sarge? Would this mean the final straw for Gavin?

Vic tapped his pen restlessly. "Well, I can get someone else."

What would a real comedienne do?

"If you let me be emcee, you can put me down as much as you want. Just don't call me Shrimp."

My smiley-face watch read 11:30 as I knocked on room 213. If I only stayed fifteen minutes I'd be home on time—no grounding, no cops, no fuming Sergeant.

But why was I here, really? It wasn't like hanging out with Cam at the club. I was meeting him in a hotel room. Maybe I was overreacting—Cam knew I had a boyfriend. But Sergeant would have a major fit if she found out. Gavin would dump me. Of course, Jazzy would be envious and tell the whole school.

"I need some ID," Cam said as he opened the door, drinking beer from a straw.

"I'm older than I look," I said as I stepped past him.

The bedspread was folded and lying neatly in the corner, replaced by a pale yellow blanket. Pens and notebooks were neatly lined up in a row on the desk. Disposable plastic cups surrounded the ice bucket where the hotel glasses should have been. His closet door was left open, revealing perfectly placed clothes on white hangers all facing the same direction.

"You must be fun on a camping trip!" I laughed.

"I bring bottled dirt! Have a seat," he said, removing a notebook from the chair. A crisp sheet covered the chair. "Want a pop?"

"Sure."

Cam opened the door.

"Where are you going?" I asked.

"To the vending machine. This isn't the Ritz."

He returned and tossed a cold Coke at me. Then he pulled out a package of straws he had in his suitcase.

"Color?" he asked.

"Yellow—to match your monogrammed towels."

He lay on his stomach on the bed and started flipping through cable channels. I sat on a hotel towel that covered the desk chairs. I was alone with an older guy in a hotel room. I reassured myself Cam wouldn't do anything improper. But had my coming given him the idea that I would?

"Sit here, it's more comfortable," he offered, tapping the bed. "Don't worry, I bring my own sheets."

"I can only stay a minute."

"I like a woman in control," he said, handing me the remote.

I flipped through the channels at a blinding pace, sitting stiffly on the edge of the bed.

Cam rested on his pillow next to me. He began stroking my hair.

"I have to get up for school tomorrow," I said, standing up.

"What are they teaching these days? Abstinence one-oh-one?"

I wasn't getting what I had come for. I wanted info on the business, but I was learning more about what a man wanted than what an audience wanted.

"Stay until the commercial," he said with begging eyes.

"Well—"

He handed me a pillow, which I held on my lap as I sat down cross-legged on the bed.

"I came to ask advice," I finally said.

"Don't bet on the Bears," Cam replied, switching to ESPN.

"I'll write that in my comedy journal."

"Go to medical school. Get married. Have three kids and get a dog."

"You sound like my mother."

"How about, don't go to strange men's hotel rooms."

"I didn't think you were a stranger."

"I'm stranger than most. But seriously, why would you want to get into this business? Spend your life living out of a suitcase, arriving at hotels that haven't received your reservation from the club that booked you, enduring a whole day alone in Spokane without a car just to spend an hour onstage? Expect to be paid five hundred dollars and be paid four? There aren't any unions to protect you. And room service doesn't deliver soul mates."

This wasn't the sort of pep talk I'd envisioned.

"Can you give me some advice about my act, Cam?"

"You're getting hired, that's the most important thing. Your act is different because of your age. There are women in this business, but not a lot. And you're funny—which doesn't hurt. Just keep performing."

I spotted the neon numbers on Cam's clock radio. 11:45. "I better go," I said, getting up.

"So soon?"

"I have school. And a prison warden at home with a Jewish accent."

"Thanks for stopping by," he said. He leaned against the door frame and stared down at me. As I looked up I could see the loneliness in his eyes.

He leaned over, but instead of kissing me on the lips, he kissed me on the cheek and hugged me tightly. I hugged him back like I didn't want to let go.

"I'll see you in Vegas," he called as I walked hurriedly down the hall.

"I'll be the wrinkled lady wearing a straw hat at the nickel slot machine," I said.

"That's not what I meant, little lady."

Jazzy and I were discussing the night's events on the front steps before school while I waited for Gavin to arrive.

"I told Vic I'd perform again," I confessed.

"But Sarge will kill you!"

"I know . . . so if he calls, should I give him an excuse?"

"Then *I'll* kill you!"

"But I made a promise to Sarge. And to Gavin."

"Heard you had a late night," Eddie interrupted as he walked up the steps.

"Ben is a bigger gossip than the *National Enquirer*," I grumbled furiously, leaning against the railing, haggard from my lack of sleep.

"Does the hip guy know about the funny guy?" he remarked, referring to Gavin and Cam.

"Sssh!" I said, nudging Eddie in the rib.

"I guess I should have gone into the hotel business instead of the pizza business," he said.

"Don't tell anyone," I warned, pinching his arm.

"Tell anyone what?" Gavin asked, walking up the steps and giving me a squeeze.

"Eddie's just jealous he's not the most hunkster guy in the Midwest."

"Just the Midwest?" Gavin asked with a grin.

"Well, okay, the world!" I exclaimed.

Eddie rolled his eyes.

"It's a drag I didn't see you perform," Gavin said. "Especially since it's over now."

Over? But it wasn't over. How could I tell Gavin?

What would he say? Would he beg for Stinkface's return?

"Well, you can now," Eddie blurted out.

"Shhh!" I whispered.

Jazzy shook her head and gave Eddie a stern stare.

"She's going to become a regular at Chaplin's!" he went on.

"No, I'm not going to be a regular," I said. "Eddie doesn't know what he's talking about!"

"You're performing again?" Gavin asked. "You didn't tell me!"

"Sorry, Trixster! I thought he'd be excited," Eddie said.

"Dork," Jazzy mumbled, pulling Eddie by the arm toward school. "See ya later."

"I was trying to tell you, Gavin."

"I thought you were finished. I thought Sarge ordered you to focus on college."

"She did. But when Vic hired me again, what could I do?"

"Say no," he offered.

"Would you say no if an architectural firm hired you?" I asked.

"No, but I wouldn't be working at eleven o'clock on a Friday night."

He pulled his hand away from mine. The bell rang. He didn't kiss or hug me good-bye. He just walked away.

I had dreamed about Gavin for two long years. And

now that we were together, I was shutting him out.

I caught up with him in the foyer. "Please come," I begged breathlessly. "Just promise to wear a blindfold and plug your ears!"

He kissed me and then left for class.

I watched as he sauntered off, his coolness oozing like steam rising from a sizzling fajita. I was Jell-O, and it wasn't even showtime.

Now I was more nervous than ever. I'd given Gavin permission to watch me tell jokes to strangers. True, he'd watched me on Open Mike, but I had been unaware of his presence that night. Now I'd be self-conscious.

What had I done?

Chaplin's microphone was slipping in my perspiring hand. Usually the audience was a sea of people, but tonight it was no bigger than a small puddle. Five audience members sat in silence as my mike shorted out.

"I loathe high school. . . ," I began. But my voice didn't carry. I continued talking, like a ventriloquist's dummy without a ventriloquist. Then abruptly the mike cut back in as I shouted, "I'm the class mime!"

No one laughed. Sweat poured down my face. The audience started booing and finally, one by one, walked out, until there was only one person left sitting alone in the back. It was Gavin. He slowly rose, walked down the aisle, shifted his

*embarrassed eyes toward me, sunk his head low, and then
walked out of the club. And my life.*

My alarm blared. I sat up, out of breath, my body
sweaty, my heart racing, adrenaline coursing through my
veins. I pounded on the snooze bar. I pulled the covers
safely over my head, wishing I had a simpler ambition —
like becoming a brain surgeon.

"We have a celebrity in the class," Mr. Janson
announced later that day.

I had quietly shared the news of my professional debut
with my dramatic mentor. If everyone hadn't known
before about my upcoming performance at Chaplin's,
they knew now. I slunk down in my chair, exhausted and
embarrassed. "Our little star is becoming a galaxy," he
declared.

I glared at Jazzy. "Make him stop."

Nathan Daniels leaned over. "Will you sign this,
Trixie?" he whispered, handing me his bus pass.
"Someday it may be worth something."

"It already is," Jazzy proclaimed.

I rolled my eyes and flipped through my comedy
notebook, hidden underneath *The Tempest.*

"The buzz is Cody Parker has made a killing making fake
IDs so kids can get into Chaplin's," Jazzy whispered to me.

"I can't perform in front of these people."

"You'll have to learn. Ricky and I are coming next Saturday night."

"No way! Promise me you won't."

"Gosh, Trix, you don't have to get so wicked. I'm your best friend. Bush people, remember?"

"You know I get nervous."

"You've invited Gavin."

"That's because I don't want to lose him."

"Well, you could lose me too."

"I'm just a beginner, Jazz. I'm not ready to perform in front of Chaplin's crowd and everyone I know. It's not like I'm Seinfeld who's been touring around the country for decades and starred in his own hit television show."

"Lighten up! No one expects you to be Seinfeld, except you. Besides, I watch the E! channel. They constantly talk about meteoric rises to fame."

All the attention was flattering, but I couldn't help it that I wasn't ready to sit on my comic comet and soar at such a rapid pace.

RISING STAR

☆

didn't have time to daydream in History, to fantasize about my beach wedding to Gavin or my debut performance on the *Douglas Douglas Show*. Not only did I have to scramble to perfect material for another week of gigs, I had the added pressure of the whole school wanting to watch me work out my kinks. I was afraid that everyone would find out that I was a fraud, that I was wasting their time on a crazy kid's pipe dream.

Anxiety forced me to focus on the most important task at hand. I scribbled jokes in my comedy notebook, hidden inside my History textbook. I muffled a laugh.

"Miss Shapiro, you seem to be buried in note taking today. May I ask you what's so funny about World War Two?"

"Excuse me?"

"What's so funny about World War Two?" Mr. Burrows repeated sternly.

"World War One was such a success, they made a sequel!"

The class roared with laughter. I had never spoken up in class before, much less not given a straight answer—especially to Mr. Burrows, whose furrowed brow and pointy ears resembled those of Beelzebub himself.

"That comment will land you in detention. You'll have all afternoon to think about history as well as your future in my class."

I had never received a scolding, or a detention. I sank in my chair, my classmates smiling at me.

"That was hilarious," Nathan Daniels whispered.

A detention slip in my hand, I was no longer the class mime. I had graduated to class clown.

Detention pushed my whole day back by two hours. I was clearing the dishes from the dinner table when Ben called me to fill in for an emcee who was stuck at the airport. Sarge agreed to let me perform that night since Ben was desperate, but only if I agreed to let her, not my dad, drop me off and pick me up, which was totally humiliating. And the detention only gave her an excuse to add more things to my To Do list. Who has time for studies, comedy, or friends when you're vacuuming a four-bedroom house?

While the audience filed into Chaplin's, I studied my Anatomy textbook instead of reviewing my comedy material.

"Veins carry the blood away from the heart and arteries carry them to it," I whispered to Ben.

"No, it's the other way around. Remember, the *a* in artery is for *away.*"

"Ugh! I'll never remember everything!"

"How do you remember all the acts you have to introduce?"

"I write them down on a little card and carry them with me onstage. I never use it. But it makes me feel secure. Like tonight," I said, pulling out a folded index card from underneath my shirt. "This has all my new material."

"There's your answer."

"That's cheating!"

"It's only cheating if you look at the card."

"Would you do it?"

"I'd cheat! I'd stick my little notecard under the desk so I could see the answers. But I'm not you. You would stick it in a place where you couldn't see it!"

I folded my index card, stuck it in my bra, and went onstage. My cheat sheet gave me so much confidence, I forgot it was even there.

I entered Anatomy class with my superstitious comfort sheet tucked into my bra. I picked up a number two pencil from Mr. Samuels' desk and quickly sat down. I glanced at the clock and thought, this is a whole lot easier than stand-up. In stand-up I only get fifteen minutes. In Anatomy, I get fifty-five.

I breezed through the test with minutes to spare and set the text on Mr. Samuels' desk. I felt something scratch my stomach.

"Are you okay, Trixie?" Mr. Samuels asked as I stood in front of the class nervously twitching.

"I just have an itch." I walked back to my desk, holding my stomach, when suddenly the notecard fell to the floor. Startled, I glanced at Mr. Samuels and tried to cover the blue card with my foot. I picked up the index card and stuck it into my back pocket.

"Trixie, can I see that?" he asked sternly.

"See what?" I asked, my heart racing.

"That card."

"Oh, my mother's grocery list? You don't want to see a boring old list. Eggs, bacon, Ben and Jerry's Chunky Monkey," I said.

"I thought I saw a diagram of a heart," he growled.

"It's a map of Whole Foods grocery. It's amazing how the frozen-food section looks just like the left ventricle."

The class snickered. But Mr. Samuels was not amused.

"But it's not what you think," I said, my hands beginning to shake.

"This really disappoints me, Trixie. You of all students!"

"I can explain the whole thing."

"You will—to me and the principal."

The only time I ever had stepped into the principal's office was when Mrs. Shuster, my tenth-grade Home Ec teacher, asked me to deliver a fresh-baked brownie to her major crush, Principal Reed. Other than that, I only saw the school leader at assemblies.

I sat outside his office, chewing my nails, as nervous as if I was about to go onstage in front of everyone I knew— without material.

Jackson Barker, the school bully, emerged with his stone-faced mother.

"Suspended. Again!" the mother grumbled as they left the waiting room.

"You may go in now," the secretary said.

I cowered in front of the principal's closed cold door, frozen.

"You'll have to open it," the secretary said.

"Oh, I thought it was automatic," I joked. But she didn't smile.

I slowly opened the creaky door and stepped inside.

"I want to see my lawyer," I demanded, anxiously sitting down in the stiff wooden chair farthest from the principal's desk.

"That won't be necessary; you're not being arrested."

"Am I being expelled? Please don't expel me!"

"Let's see what's in your file," he said, opening a manila folder. "Well, the truth is, there isn't much here. Before last month's illness, you had perfect attendance."

"I was grounded by my mother for staying out too late."

"This isn't confession, Trixie."

"I didn't cheat, Principal Reed. I didn't look at the index card. Ask any of the kids sitting next to me. It wasn't a cheat sheet, but a comfort sheet—like a baby blanket. A soft pink one, with ventricles."

Principal Reed leered at me curiously over his bifocals as I rattled on. "See, I work at Chaplin's and when I have to memorize my material I make a list and stick it into my bra. Can I say that word in front of you? I never take the card out to look at it," I continued. "I don't need to, but it comforts me."

I had argued my case with clarity and passion. Now I had to wait to see if I'd convinced the judge. The second hand on the wall clock ticked loudly as the principal fingered my model-thin file.

"Well, Mr. Samuels did mention it seemed out of character for you. What's this about Chaplin's?"

"I perform stand-up."

"At your age?" he asked, surprised.

"Mr. Janson got me started."

"My wife loves stand-up."

"I can get you in free. Uh—I don't mean that as a bribe! Am I going to be expelled?"

"You have to retake the test in my office tomorrow after school. Without extra padding!"

"That's a good one! If you're interested, Open Mike is Monday."

I stood alone, onstage. The young audience had wide eyes but no mouths. How would they be able to laugh? I tried to tell a joke, but my words were muffled and trapped. I put my hand to my mouth and realized my mouth was gone. I only felt a jaw and smooth flesh. I tried to scream, but my voice was a muffled echo in my head. The teenage crowd grew restless and hostile as I tried to spit my words out. Frustrated, they began throwing textbooks at me—History, Anatomy, Algebra 2.

I tried everything to win their approval. I tap-danced, I mimed walking up a ladder, I juggled Magic 8 Balls. As the balls landed in my hands, the magic pyramid that normally floated to the glass surface of the ball, revealing a fortune in the words Yes, No, or Ask again later, appeared instead with images. One ball revealed Gavin's face, one Sarge's, while the third showed Jazzy. I desperately tried to keep them from crashing to the stage.

"I can't keep up!" I screamed aloud, to the shock and horror of my English Lit class.

My face and neck were stiff from sleeping on my desk. The other students gawked at me.

"It seems as though you can't keep awake either," Mr. Harris said. "You might at least pretend you're interested."

I looked for comfort from Jazzy, who sat in the front row pointing to my cheek. Confused, I raised my hand to my face and felt an indentation along my cheek where I'd been branded by my spiral binder.

The class continued to laugh as I slunk in my chair.

Sometimes the attention you receive isn't the attention you seek.

"It's been forever since we've hung out," Jazzy said, driving me home from school. "Let's stop at the mall. Bloomie's is having a sale on nail polish. Unless you need another nap," she teased.

"I can't. I have homework."

"Man, Trix, we never do anything anymore."

"I'll hang with you next week."

"Next week? That's forever!"

"I promise, we'll shop till we max out our credit cards, okay?"

"You'll have an excuse for copping out then, as well. Too tired. Too much homework. A show. You're becoming a total crankmeister."

"What do you want from me?"

"Some girlie hang time. Kick back. Buy some new ear-rings. All work and no play makes Trixie a very dull girl."

I rolled my eyes and sighed. "I can't be everything to everybody."

"You sound like an Oprah New Age guru. I'm just say-ing I miss us."

"I do too. I couldn't survive high school without you, but—"

I looked at Jazzy. She looked back.

I couldn't lose my best friend. Not after everything we'd been through.

"Well, not more than one hour," I said, giving in.

"Blitzen, babe! I knew you'd come around," she said, changing lanes. "We'll tell Sarge I had to stop for an oil change."

The next day I was in the rest room washing my sweaty palms after completing my Anatomy test under the scrutiny of Principal Reed's bifocals, when I heard a breathy voice from one of the stalls. "I got my fake ID, so I can go to Chaplin's with you Friday after the game."

"I can't wait," another girl answered. "It'll be nice to see someone else sweat besides football players for a change."

"Who'd have thought? I didn't know that mousey girl had a voice box."

"She must have more than a voice box to be going out with Gavin."

Just then two toilets flushed and out stepped two varsity cheerleaders in blue-and-gold uniforms. They scrubbed their hands before noticing me rummaging through my purse in front of the mirror.

I thought they might harrass me or flush my head in the toilet. But instead, they looked at me as if they had just spotted a movie star.

"Oh—this is totally fab! Trixie Shapiro! I can't believe you're in here!" shouted Amber Hammond.

"We're coming to see you Friday," Jenny Larson added.

"We never see you at the games."

"She's probably busy practicing her comedy, stupid," Jenny said. "I'm having a party on the fourth. You have to come."

"Yes, you must. You can tell some jokes," Amber suggested.

"I always thought you were totally cool. Promise me you'll come," Jenny said.

I was shocked. I was being invited to a party? By cheerleaders!

I'd always dreamed of this moment—to be invited to

parties by cheerleaders. But where had these Glam Girls been the last three years? Should I decline their invitation? I did like the attention and I'd always wanted to know what the "in" crowd was doing while Jazzy and I had been home, girl-talking. So I nodded eagerly.

Jenny opened the door and Amber followed after. "I can't believe she was in . . . there," Amber whispered.

"I guess she has to pee like everyone else," Jenny said, and they both giggled as the door shut behind them.

Later that night I was watching *The Simpsons* and writing a new joke in my comedy notebook when Sarge called from the kitchen, "Don't forget, your cousin Lanie is getting married this weekend. I want your bags packed by Thursday at the latest."

I was shocked. She couldn't be talking about this weekend.

"I thought I told you to get rid of that book," Sarge hollered, marching into the living room.

"I can't go to the wedding," I confessed, having completely forgotten about Lanie. Gavin, Jazzy, Chaplin's, homework, tests—it was enough to remember my own name!

"You have to go," Sarge demanded, heading for the dining room.

"But, Ma . . . I have plans," I confessed.

"Then an emergency divorce!"

Sarge glared at me.

"What would Lanie do if she had a professional commitment?"

"I guess she'd have to miss your wedding."

"See! Her situation is no different from mine."

"But, Trixie," my mother began sternly, "that's her profession!"

I froze. Steam was building up from the soles of my gym shoes to the purple barrettes in my hair.

"And this is mine!" I declared, clutching my comedy notebook.

Sarge was startled at my sudden outburst.

"This is mine!" I shouted dramatically at the top of my lungs. I ran upstairs to the safety of my room.

"You're too young to have a profession!"

Tears streaming down my face, I slammed the door. My mirror shook. Pictures of comedians on my wall billowed from the gust of wind.

I'd run away only one time in my life. I had been seven and had packed a backpack with a tuna sandwich and my Hello Kitty doll. I'd known I wanted to run away but hadn't known where to go. I'd sulked next to our crooked swing in my backyard. I'd waited for Sarge to scream, "Where's my baby?" I had waited for the police cars. The only sign of life I had seen was the ruffling of my parents' bedroom curtains.

Starving, I had eaten my sandwich. Then I'd gone back inside and thrown my backpack on my bed. I had run away for one whole hour.

This time I was brought back to reality as I was shoving underwear into my suitcase, wiping tears of sadness and anger off my cheeks, when there was a knock at the door.

"I'm not here!" I shouted.

The door squeaked open.

"You'll write?" Dad asked, eyeing the suitcase.

"I can't live with that woman in a house where I can't explore my passion," I cried. "She's standing in the way of all that I've ever dreamed of! I am an artist. I need to be free to paint my canvases!"

"She just wants what's best for you," he said, sitting at my desk chair. "I want what's best for you too. Only your mother and I don't agree what that is."

"You don't?" I asked, surprised.

My dad was the silent type, but when he spoke—his words carried the weight of thunder, the power of Gandhi, the authority of the president.

"I think you have something, and your mother and I would be foolish to stand in your way."

"Really?" I asked.

"I've always thought you were funny. But you're my little girl, so I may be biased. Still, when you win a contest and professional bookers are paying you to entertain in their club—then you need to explore what's being offered. It's not your mother's—or my—dream you need to live. It's your dream. "

Wow. His words melted my anger away. My bleak future seemed to have a rainbow. "So I can still live here?"

"I never said you couldn't."

"But I can still perform?"

"You have to keep your grades up. And you're still too young to walk home alone at night. In fact, you're never walking home at night—even when you're fifty."

"What about the wedding?" I asked, with reservation.

"Your mother can attend alone. It's her side of the family anyway," he said with a wink.

"Of course! Thanks, Dad!" I exclaimed, dropping my suitcase with a thud and squeezing him with all my might. "Who's going to tell Sarge?" I asked him as he headed for the door.

"Who do you think?" he asked smugly.

"If you need the suitcase, it's already packed!"

The next morning Sarge was the silent one. The clanging of dishes was the only noise I heard while I quickly downed a blueberry Pop-Tart. Unfortunately the silence wore off when Jazzy picked me up for school.

"Your room needs to be straightened before you go out tonight," Sarge nagged.

"I think I prefer her when she's mad," I whispered to Jazzy as I shut the door behind me.

It was Wednesday, opening night of my week-long run at Chaplin's, and Dad drove me to the event.

"Knock 'em dead!" he said in the car.

"I'll try."

"Here," he said, handing me a Mickey Mantle gold coin. "For good luck."

"Thanks," I said, hugging him hard. I stuck the coin in my shoe and waved as I ran inside.

I was terrified. Now every student with a fake ID at Mason could pay to watch me bomb.

I approached Ben, who was counting reservations at the ticket booth.

"Memorize this," I said, plopping down last year's Mason yearbook.

"You're joking!"

"Gavin, Jazzy, and the whole school are coming. But since they're underage, you won't be able to let them enter. Comprende?"

Ben started flipping through the yearbook. He seemed particularly occupied with the cheerleading pictures.

"Just remember you could get fired and Vic could lose

his liquor license if you serve to minors."

"Are you really concerned I'll lose my job, or am I sensing stage fright?"

"I don't want you to end up homeless," I said coyly.

"No one without wrinkles gets in," he finally promised, taking another peek at the cheerleaders.

But he kept his word and, as I later found out, tried to turn away a thirty-year-old woman with braces.

By Friday night's midnight show, I hadn't been late to school once. I had also managed to spend a little time with Jazzy and Gavin and had completed all my homework.

Cam, Tucker, and I had just finished the eight thirty show when it seemed like we were starting another one again.

I was exhausted. My legs were so tense, they felt like tree trunks on quicksand, the microphone like a skyscraper in my hand. My brain was so fried, I'd written the intros on a paper and laid it, along with a pencil and Mountain Dew, next to the stool. I was afraid if I didn't have caffeine I'd pass out.

I delivered my first punch line to lazy chuckles. The patrons mumbled to one another and ordered their drinks loudly from the waitresses.

All at once I became lost in my set. Hadn't I already said

"class mime"? I'd said that joke once on Thursday's show, and twice before this week. But did I say it twice just now? Where was I? The beginning of my routine or the end?

I peeked at my watch, realizing I'd only been onstage for two minutes. I was at the beginning! I had to perform for thirteen more minutes! The audience was ignoring me and I was weary and couldn't remember my next line. Even if I embellished Cam's and Tucker's credits, I would still need to fill ten minutes.

I felt trapped in the cigarette smoke, which permeated the room like fog in a black-and-white horror flick. The audience resembled zombies, staring with blank expressions. I stared back in horror.

My routine became like a drunken friend, trying to walk home, stumbling, bumbling, slurring words, blurting out the wrong words. And I still had seven minutes to go. Minutes are like light-years when you are bombing. My hair was turning gray by the second.

Suddenly I burst out, "My mom's such a control freak . . . she goes to a furniture store and rearranges the furniture!"

What did I just say? I'd planned to say that as my last joke. Where the hell was I? What could I say next?

My pain was so obvious that the audience became self-conscious, afraid to break the silence with any noise, much less laughter.

I could feel them feeling sorry for me.

Then I spotted Cam in the back of the house, drinking his beer through a straw, watching me with a calm expression, even a smile. Suddenly I recalled him once saying, "You have the mike, not them."

It was as if I now had the confidence Cam always had.

"Well, people," I began matter-of-factly. "I've got five more minutes up here and if you guys want to talk amongst yourselves, go ahead. But I came here to have fun. So I'm going to sing a song."

Suddenly the audience came alive.

"Whoo!" a table shouted. Others started applauding. "Sing, baby, sing!"

"Take it off too!" I heard a voice call.

"You go, girl!" another voice chimed in.

Growing up, I'd practiced my own songs in my room for the *Trixie Shapiro Show*. I wasn't ready to perform them onstage, but at this point it was either sing or die.

I placed the mike in the stand, removed my drink and intro paper from the stool, and slipped the weathered pencil into my pocket. I walked back to the mike with complete confidence. I could sense Cam and Ben from the back of the house wondering what I was doing.

"I'd like to sing a simple love song to a very special friend of mine," I began. "And this little number," I sang, holding up the pencil, "is for my Number . . . Two!"

The audience came to life. I began singing.

> *I met you at school,*
>
> *It really was fate,*
>
> *You were my paper mate,*
>
> *You're my Number Two . . .*

The audience roared as I took a deep breath and sang on.

> *From my ABCs to our SATs,*
>
> *You're not a Hi-Liter,*
>
> *But you made my day brighter,*
>
> *You're my Number Two . . .*
>
> *Now computers are here,*
>
> *It's not like preschool year,*
>
> *We were together every day,*
>
> *Now laptops are in our way,*
>
> *You're my Number Two!*

Then I revved up and belted out:

> *Now no one writes letters,*
>
> *They say e-mail is better.*
>
> *But I prefer your eraser*
>
> *To hitting the backspacer,*
>
> *You're my Number Two . . .*

You'll always be near,

Right behind my ear,

You're my Number Two.

Then I pleaded to the audience,

Don't leave him for dead,

'Cause he's filled with . . .

"Lead!" the audience finished.

He got me through elementary school,

He was my favorite tool,

He's my Number Two.

You're . . .

"My Number Two," we all sang in unison.

The audience burst into applause. The front row even gave me a standing ovation.

I was euphoric, triumphant. Bursting with electricity. I ran offstage and over to Cam.

"That was hilarious—I didn't know you could sing. Why haven't you done that before? It killed!" he exclaimed.

"Are you kidding? It killed me!" I said, and plopped into my seat exhausted, realizing how close I had come to a complete fiasco. "I'm never performing again."

★　★　★

I spent Saturday afternoon with Gavin at Take One Cinema.

I tried to pay attention to *The Incinerator*, while the teenagers in the movie were screaming as they tried to escape the clutches of the psycho "Incinerator" who wanted to use them instead of charcoal, but not even that could keep me awake. I rested my head on Gavin's shoulder and fell asleep.

"Time to go," I heard him say.

Disoriented, I wiped my eyes. The credits were rolling. "Great film," I mumbled.

"Yeah, the credits get four stars!"

For years I'd fantasized about seeing a movie with Gavin and now that it had actually happened, I was a struggling narcoleptic.

He was annoyed and walked ahead. I caught up to him as he threw the popcorn in the lobby trash.

"I only have three more shows. Then I'm free to be your love slave forever!"

Even though I still wanted to be a stand-up comic, I knew there wasn't another Gavin Baldwin in the whole wide world and I didn't want to lose him.

The next night Ben slacked off in the ID department.

"How'd you get in?" I scolded Jazzy, who was comfortably sitting at a stage-side table with Ricky.

"Eddie's brother likes blondes," she said with a smirk.

"You'll be fabulous," Jazzy said, patting my arm.

"But I completely bombed last night."

"Get out! Ben told me you rocked the house like Tina Turner!"

"Only at the end, and only by accident. Did Gavin sneak in too?" I asked, eyeballing the crowd.

"He doesn't have to. He's eighteen."

"I know, but he's still illegal here. They have his mug shot out front."

"Speaking of mug shots, I saw your photo in the lobby with the other comedians. You look so glam!"

"Jazzy, please sit in the back, way in the back—like maybe in the alley."

I retreated to my usual table, frustrated and nervous. Hopefully the stage lights would blind me from seeing Jazzy and Ricky. But to be safe, I decided I'd only deliver my material to the middle section of the audience. In the meantime I bit my nails and twirled my hair until my name was called.

"And here's Trixie Shapiro!" Ben announced offstage.

I ran up the aisle and stepped onstage. I grabbed the microphone and gazed above the crowd, not making eye contact.

"My boyfriend and I slept together at the movie theater," I began. Male audience members hooped and hollered. "Yep . . . Pauly Shore starred in another picture!"

The audience laughed.

"Anybody here on a date?" I continued.

"I am!" Jazzy said, waving her hand wildly.

Jazzy? She wasn't supposed to respond. How could I improvise with someone I already knew? Normally I would ask, "Where are you from?" But I already knew the answer. I clutched the microphone with all my might. My hands started to perspire. "Where did the two of you meet?" I imagined myself asking. "At Eddie's party!" Jazzy would say. "You know that, Trixie!"

I twisted my hair, gazing blankly at my best friend. What could I say? I was losing my material again, just like at Talent Night. But this time I'd get an F for "Fired!"

"How long have you been dating?" I imagined asking. "Duh, Trixie, we're best friends!" Jazzy would answer in front of the whole audience. "Best friends" would echo over and over, making me feel like I was a traveling medicine man whose Fountain of Youth elixir is revealed to be lemonade. I shifted back and forth, obsessively fingering my hair and staring hypnotically at Jazzy. What could I say?

"Yes," she repeated. "I'm on a date!"

"He's very handsome; does he have a brother?" I finally asked, frozen.

"No, but I can be available after I drop her off!" Ricky shouted back. The audience laughed and Jazzy slugged him in the arm.

I had to make a decision. Freeze, or take back control. This was my job—a fifteen-minute one—and I had to be a professional. I couldn't choke again. It was my stage and my audience, and I needed to shun my best friend to keep her from torpedoing my act.

I quickly turned my attention away from her.

"Are you on a date?" I asked an older couple, seated on the opposite side of the stage.

"No, we're married," the woman answered.

"Wow, a date that you have to pay for—for the rest of your life!"

The couple and the audience laughed. I delivered the next set of my material to the right side of the stage and then I turned to the left side, only I focused above the heads of the audience. I went back into my routine and ignored Jazzy and Ricky for the rest of the show. I completely concentrated on making a connection with the whole audience, and forgetting the individual patter. After a while, I forgot they were there—until the show was over.

"You're a star!" Jazzy proclaimed, squeezing my hand with all her might.

"You weren't supposed to talk—I almost lost everything."

"Relax! You were great. And that Tucker guy was filthy! I loved it."

"I know, that's why I can't let Sarge here. She thinks Chaplin's bleeps comics' language like they do on Comedy Central."

"You totally stoked," Ricky said, squeezing me tight.

"You got a laugh yourself," I replied. "You should try Open Mike—"

"No way. Being a smart-ass is one thing, but getting up in front of all those people is quite another."

Audience members congratulated me while the waitresses emptied ashtrays and the guests arriving for the second show streamed in.

"You're so totally Comedy Central," Jazzy said, nudging me.

Suddenly my dark-haired hipster walked into the room, along with Sam Chapman.

"Tell him I didn't invite you!" I whispered to Jazzy.

"Well, Trix," Jazzy improvised. "Here's the two dollars Sarge asked me to drop off for you in case of emergency. Lucky we were in the neighborhood." Jazzy left mouthing the words, "You were awesome."

"I'm turning white," I whispered to Gavin. "Jazzy spoke to me during my set and I was this close to blanking out," I said, inching my thumb and finger together.

"Do I know you?" Gavin asked dramatically.

"Gavin, I'm freaking out," I confessed. "I'm panicking.

Would you mind coming tomorrow?"

"Do you know this girl?" Gavin asked Sam.

"Never seen her before in my life," Sam replied.

"I just need more time. Please, I'll leave you tickets for tomorrow," I begged.

"Come here often?" Gavin asked.

"After this show, I guarantee I'll never be back."

"I've heard it's hard for some comics to perform in front of their friends. Are you a comic, or a waitress?"

"VIPs get to sit in the front, plebeians in the kitchen next to the emergency exit. I'd love to stay and chat, but I have to find a substitute for tonight's show."

"Hey, sugar," Gavin called as I started to leave. "Can I get some curly fries and your number?"

"As a matter of fact you can. Because after this show I'm going to be dumped by my boyfriend!"

I frantically left for the bathroom.

I stood in front of the mirror, terrified. I didn't want to perform. What if every punch line was delivered into dead air? What if my song didn't save me this time?

I took a deep breath. "I've performed before, many times now," I told myself, "and I've performed in front of Janson, Ben, and now Jazzy and Ricky. I can do this! I've got to. For me and for Gavin."

I hurried out, feeling braver now. Several audience

members were straggling into the theater. But Gavin was standing in the hallway with Sam. He wasn't smiling.

"Hey listen," he said, distracted, his hands in his pockets. "Me and Sam are going to head over to his house for poker."

"I'll leave you tickets for tomorrow? It's my last show."

"Thanks, but that's okay. I'm busy."

"Well . . . ," I began, feeling a knot in my stomach. "I can come by before the show?"

"I've got things—"

"After the show?"

"Listen, I gotta run."

My heart sank. He was leaving. Really leaving! Was he leaving for good? The thought was pure torture. I was getting what I had wished for, but not in the way I had wished.

"No, don't go. I'll be okay, really," I begged. "Just sit in the back."

"'Bye," he said, opening the front door.

"Gavin!" I called, running over to him.

But he pulled away without a kiss, without a hug. Without a word.

My heart stopped.

"Gavin, please don't go! Please don't go! Not like this!" I yelled into the parking lot. "Please don't leave like this!"

"Trixie, you're on!" Ben called.

"You can't keep letting hecklers in here," I scolded, wiping a tear from my welling eyes. "They ruin the show."

I awoke the next morning thinking, as always, of Gavin. But today my heart felt different. It felt empty.

I immediately picked up the phone.

"No, he's not here," his father said.

"Do you know when he'll be back?"

"He said he'd be gone all day."

"All day?" But it was only eleven o'clock. I couldn't wait all day! "Can you tell him Trixie called?"

"Yes, Trixie."

I paged Gavin, left a note on his e-mail and a message on his voice mail.

I jumped every time the phone rang and growled when it was for Sarge.

Jazzy stopped by later, after a day at the mall with her mom. "What are you still doing in your pajamas?" she wondered, finding me sluffed out on the couch.

"He hates me!" I wailed, explaining in frantic detail the previous night's events. "I've called him seven times, but his father keeps saying he's out getting his oil changed. He's probably with Stinkface."

"Maybe he's really getting his oil changed."

"He left the show, Jazz! I've never had anyone walk out during a show, much less before the show."

"I'm sure it's not—"

"What do I do?" I pleaded. "He's never looked at me like that. I hurt him to his core. I've totally blown it." I sank my head into a pillow.

"You're not throwing in the towel without a fight," Jazzy said, grabbing the pillow. "Am I talking to the same girl I met in the school bushes?"

"What do you do when you and Ricky fight?"

"I dress up in my red dress and heels. Then suddenly he's begging to make up."

"Yeah, but what can I do? All I own is a pair of tap shoes." I pulled a white afghan over my head in despair. "I surrender."

"We'll fix you up!" Jazzy said, and dragged me upstairs.

"Remember I have a show tonight," I said, sitting help-lessly on the bed. "I don't have time for a makeover."

Jazzy scrambled through my dresser drawers and closet. "What's this?" she asked, pulling out a black dress in the shape of a tent.

"My aunt Sylvia bought it for me."

"Well, Aunt Sylvia, your niece goes to high school, not a senior center. Close your eyes, Trix—this may get ugly."

Jazzy grabbed a pair of scissors from my desk and cut off the collar and sleeves, then tucked under the frayed ends and secured them with Scotch tape. She then placed black tights and high-heeled funky boots underneath the dress. "Now it looks killer!"

I stared at the spontaneous haute couture creation in her hands.

"Make sure to spray your hair," Jazzy dictated as I slid into the outfit. "When does Sarge get home?"

"Midnight."

"You'll have plenty of time to make up or make out, however you want to put it," she said, zipping me up.

I examined myself in the mirror.

"I look like a slut," I said, turning from side to side. I stared at my reflection, which had been transformed from teeny bopper to sex kitten.

"I promise Gavin will be begging for an encore," said Jazzy.

What am I doing? I thought, as I drove my mom's car through the twinkling snow after Chaplin's Sunday show—a fresh two hundred dollars in my purse and another week's work penciled in on my calendar. I had one hour until my mom's plane returned. I was determined to get Gavin back, and have some fun in the process.

"Whoa!" Gavin said, opening his bedroom door.

I was in my hot dress, a scarf dangling seductively from my neck.

"I have an invitation," I said in a breathy whisper.

"But your show is over."

"No, not to the show!"

"To dinner at Maggiano's?"

"To dessert!"

"We'll have dessert here," he said, closing his door and pulling me onto his bed.

Since our relationship consisted of hanging out at school and going to parties, I hadn't had the pleasure of seeing the inside of Gavin's house. But I knew the outside of 2400 Gettys Lane by heart, after spending two years begging Jazzy to drive out of our way so I could gaze at his magical dwelling. Now I was the uninvited guest, and the host might possibly hate my guts.

I walked up the long driveway and rang the Baldwins' bell, bundled in my puffy down coat. I looked like I was going to retrieve my dogsled rather than my angry boyfriend.

Would Gavin shut the door on me? Would he tell me to go away? Would he still pretend he didn't know me? I heard the sound of a barking dog—how appropriate.

The rustic red door opened. It wasn't Gavin—it was Mr. Baldwin. A handsome specimen in brown-leather house shoes. Jazzy's plan hadn't mentioned parents. I wanted to turn around and go home and call the whole seduction off.

"I must have the wrong house," I said apologetically.

"Don't I know you?" Mr. Baldwin asked, confused.

"We've never met, but I've spoken to you on the phone."

"Ahh . . . yes. A friend of Gavin's?"

"I'm Trixie."

"Of course. Trixie, c'mon in."

"I feel terrible arriving so late."

"Don't be silly. We're all still up. Gavin! You have company!"

I was freezing, my tiny head and skinny legs poking out of my purple down coat. I didn't look like a sex kitten, I looked like the Blueberry Girl from *Willy Wonka*.

I patted their neurotic jumping Yorkshire terrier with my purple-mittened hand as Gavin raced down the stairs.

"Oh . . . hi," he said with reservation.

Suddenly a jet-black-haired Martha Stewart entered the room.

"Hi," Mrs. Baldwin said.

"Mom and Dad, this is Trixie," he said. "Trixie, this is my mom and dad."

"It's nice to meet you, Mr. and Mrs. Baldwin."

"So you're Trixie," Mrs. Baldwin said. "Glad to put a face to the voice. Can I take your coat?"

"No!" I blurted out. "I mean, no thanks!"

I had dreamed about meeting Mr. and Mrs. Baldwin

ever since that first smile from Gavin over two years ago. Eating cranberry sauce at Thanksgiving dinner, chatting at a backyard barbecue, taking pictures of us on prom night. But not around for a seduction! "I can't stay long. I'm sorry I arrived so late."

"That's okay. We'll leave you be," his mom said.

I felt something itching my leg. The taped hem was starting to unravel and was poking me in the thigh. My nouveau-*Cosmo* dress was quickly resembling something out of the Flintstones. I sat on the Baldwins' leather couch with my coat zipped up to my chin.

All I could do was pray that the puffy coat cushioned the fall when Gavin finally dumped me for good.

Gavin was wearing a worn Radiohead T-shirt and black boxers, and was barefoot. He was gorgeous. He sat on the ottoman staring at the fireplace while I fiddled with the zipper on my coat—neither of us saying a word.

"Aren't you hot?" he asked finally.

"I'm still cold from outside."

"Want something warm to drink?"

"I really should go," I said, rising.

"Have a seat. I'll get you some hot chocolate."

I guess he felt better dumping me over cocoa and marshmallows.

When he went into the kitchen, I unzipped my coat and checked the damage. I quickly tucked the unraveling tape back into the dress. I zipped up when I heard Gavin's footsteps.

"Thanks." I sipped the hot chocolate. Steam rose from the cup, making my face even more flushed than it already was. We sat in silence again. I was crumbling inside.

"It's a good thing you left last night," I began. "The show sucked!"

Gavin fingered his watch.

"But I bet you had a great poker game."

"I lost twenty bucks."

"How 'bout that oil change?" I hinted.

"The oil was the least of it. I needed a new muffler."

"You really got your oil changed? Jazzy and I use that as our excuse with Sarge. So I just thought . . ."

Gavin wrinkled his forehead.

"I just needed practice. I want to put on a great show for you, and at this point I'm just trying to stand up there without forgetting my material, trying not to shake too much and to make the audience laugh. If you're there, then I have to worry about pleasing you too."

"But I already saw you on Open Mike and you killed!"

"But I didn't know you were there—or I would have froze."

How could I tell him that I still counted his smiles, that he made my knees weak and my hormones soar? I didn't want to sound crazy.

"It would be like performing for the king," I finally admitted.

"You mean Elvis?"

"I was thinking of a king of a country!" I said.

"I'm not a king," he exclaimed, laughing.

"But to me you are. Don't you get it?"

"No—"

"I've been crushed out on you for two years!"

"Two years?" he asked, suddenly flattered.

"Duh! Wasn't it written all over my geeky face?"

"You're not a geek! But two years?"

"I never knew I'd be sitting here—in Gavin Baldwin's house. Or that I'd ever be performing at Chaplin's. I just need a little time, that's all. Everything has happened so fast."

"Yeah . . . I guess we've really only been going out for a couple of weeks. It just seems like we've been together longer."

"Do you mean that in a good way?"

He nodded. "You think differently from other girls. I'm not used to dating someone who wants more from life than a makeover."

"Thanks," I said, beaming.

"And you think differently from me," he confessed.

"But I don't want to be different from you," I said,

feeling a lonely pang.

"Why? You follow your dream," he replied.

"So do you. You're going to be an architect."

"That's my father's dream," he whispered. "Being practical."

"Then what is yours?"

He half laughed. "No one's ever asked me that before."

"Well . . ."

"I don't have a dream."

"There is nothing you're passionate about?"

"Those lips," he said, looking at my mouth.

I smiled. "But really."

"I've always wanted to write," he said, thoughtful.

"Nothing's stopping you—"

"There's a lot of things stopping me."

"Just yourself."

"Anyway," he said, changing his tone. "I admire your courage to go onstage. And to come here."

I felt my heart melt inside.

"But I'm chicken when it comes to performing in front of you. Come to Chaplin's as soon as my set is over," I began. "And watch hilarious touring professional middles and headliners. I'll get you in for free and we'll sit together. I'll introduce you to any comic you want to meet."

"Bernie Mac?" he asked, excited.

"I don't think he's played Chaplin's for years."

"It was cool you came over. It took guts." Gavin sat next to me on the couch.

Then he leaned over and kissed me. "Why don't you take off that coat," he suggested.

I glanced at my watch. It was 11:30. "I have to go! Sarge and Dad will be home any minute."

"You have something on your leg," he said as I reached the door.

"Oh, it's—," but he had already tugged at it. He ended up with a fistful of tape as my dress unraveled.

"It was Jazzy's idea!" I said, embarrassed.

"Isn't everything Jazzy's idea?"

"I wanted you back."

"You could have just said, 'Sorry.'"

"Sorry? That's all I had to do?"

"It wasn't all your fault. You needed space. That's cool. . . . I should have respected that. I just wanted to see you shine."

I hugged him tight.

I couldn't wait to tell Jazzy I had made up with Gavin without even taking off my coat. I drove home, the snow softly hitting the windshield like tiny kisses.

FATHER KNOWS BEST

☆

One night, during the headliner's set, I grabbed my purse and bolted for a bathroom break. I opened the theater doors into the lobby and bumped into a man in a Big Bob's baseball cap and sunglasses. "Excuse me," I said and raced off.

"You dropped this, Trix," a familiar voice said. The man picked up my hairbrush, which had dropped to the floor.

I slowly turned around as the oddly dressed man retreated and tried to escape back into the club.

This couldn't be happening.

"Dad?"

"You must be mistaken," the man muttered in a deep voice.

"How'd you get in here?" I asked, puzzled. "You're supposed to meet me at the bar when I'm done."

"I . . . uh . . ."

"And why are you wearing that stupid hat? You never wear hats!"

"I was . . . cold?"

"You snuck in tonight?" I asked condescendingly.

"Well . . . yes."

"You know that's forbidden!" And then it dawned on me. "Don't tell me you've always been here!"

"Of course not. The bar has a TV—sometimes I watch the Bears."

"I don't believe you."

"I slip in when they call your name and watch from the kitchen till you run onstage at the end of the show," he confessed, proud of his scheme.

"It sounds like something I'd do," I said, remembering the Varicose Veins concert. "But what about the four-letter words and blue humor some of the headliners use?" I asked, alarmed.

"Nothing I haven't heard Sid say," he said.

"But this was my private thing. Didn't you trust me?"

"Of course. But you work in . . . a bar."

"It's a comedy club, Dad, not a strip club!"

"And you're only seventeen."

"Only? In Tibet I could rule a country."

"I'm sorry, Trix. If you were a father, you'd understand."

"If you were a teenager, you'd understand."

I was totally conflicted. As much as I felt betrayed, I also felt like I had a guardian angel who had patiently stood back to let me fly on my own, but kept an eye out so I didn't crash into a tree.

Ben poked his head out the theater door. "Trixie, Frank's almost done. You've gotta do closing announcements."

"Your act improves all the time," my dad said assuredly.

"You think?"

"I know."

It was nice to know he'd seen me perform at something beyond Talent Night.

"And your mother . . . ," he whispered.

"Sarge? At Chaplin's? How could you?" I whined.

"How could I keep her away? She was so proud of you!"

"But I would have heard her coming a mile away!"

"Well, her disguise was better than mine. She wore a cook's uniform and watched with me from the kitchen. She was only here once, though. She saw you perform and then got banned when Vic found her trying to fire the cook."

Ben poked his head out again and anxiously said, "Trixie, let's go!"

"But I didn't get to pee!"

"Hey," said Dad. "Watch your language!"

"See, this is why fathers aren't allowed. If you heckle me—I'll throw you out personally," I said with a grin.

★ ★ ★

From then on Dad sat hidden in the back of the house with a bowl of peanuts within arm's reach. He became an armchair comedian. On the short ride home he'd give me friendly advice. During the day I started to run new jokes by him. We rented DVDs of comedians and dissected their jokes and performances. We'd review my videotapes at Chaplin's and analyze what worked, what didn't, and why. My act began improving at a rapid pace.

SPECIAL GUEST

☆

C hicago's windchill factor had calmed, and overcast skies were replaced with vanilla cotton ball clouds and blue sky. Spring. The biggest decision of a student's life was rolling near—college. Where did I want to go? Did I want to go? What did I want to major in? What were my goals?

Gavin and Jazzy applied to Northwestern—Gavin for architecture, and Jazzy for marketing. To me college was just high school that you had to pay for. However, since my parents had a glimpse of comics struggling on the road, they insisted I had to have something to fall back on—at least a liberal arts education. I had no natural desire to go to a university, but I wanted to be near Gavin, Jazzy, and Chaplin's. Northwestern had a beautiful campus and was on Lake Michigan.

And if I didn't fill out the application, Sergeant would.

The next four months my dreams continued to come true, but I was always afraid they would unravel at any moment and I'd wake up in the morning without a boyfriend or a stage to perform on—back to the same person I'd been when those seniors threw me into a bush with Jazzy.

I kept in touch with Cam through e-mail while he traveled the road to Denver, Phoenix, Milwaukee, Louisville, and New York. He encouraged me to hit other clubs too. Local comics from Chaplin's suggested other open mikes. Soon Dad began schlepping me to Evanston's Holiday Inn and downtown Chicago's Bar None. Vic even booked me to emcee a corporate party. I took every gig I could get, every open mike where I could perform.

It was nice to receive compliments every night and make new friends, which had always been a challenge for the shy me. Many things that had always been difficult now came more easily, even performing. I still bombed occasionally, but was able to shrug off the bad performances as I realized it was more a lack of chemistry with the audience than my material. And my material, my delivery, and my confidence were progressing from week to week.

It was during this time that I stopped dreaming about star-shaped pools and Hollywood parties. My mind didn't have time to wander, as all my energy was spent juggling homework, writing new material, performing, and dating

Gavin. My lavish fantasy bedroom reverted to the reality of a tiny room strewn with dirty clothes, and sheets I didn't have time to change. Instead of being a Glam Girl when I saw Gavin, I had to mask the bags that began making a permanent home underneath my eyes.

As for school, I don't know how I managed to keep up my grades and near perfect attendance—maybe it was the three cups of coffee I downed every morning and the Power Bars I ate for lunch. My minor celebrity status, which had initially seemed temporary, was now taken for granted by my classmates and teachers. Even Mr. Owens began referring to me as "The Comedienne."

At home, Sarge seemed resigned to my new career, my late nights, the smell of smoke on my clothes—but she still made me do the dishes. As for my dad, it's ironic that a disguise brought us closer together and I saw qualities in him that I had never known existed. He was very creative. He could spot a bad joke coming before the punch line was said. He saw an "off" night as a challenge to turn into an "on" night. He was patient during the late-night drives and enthusiastic when everything clicked. I think I was as much surprised by the changes in him as he was by the changes in me.

Finally there was Gavin. Still in my life, working on smile number 1,006 . . . 1,007? . . . When did I stop counting? I somehow made time for Saturday matinees,

Sunday videos, and kissing sessions before study hall. But seeing him every day and walking with his arm around me didn't lessen my awe of him, or the fear I felt of losing him every time a cheerleader looked his way.

"Does this look luscious or what?" Jazzy said, modeling a navy-blue prom dress in Groovy Garments' fitting room. "It says fun, inviting, sexy!" She twirled around as if she was a prom angel. "Now you."

"I hate mine," I scoffed, wearing a puffy pink taffeta dress. "It looks like a tablecloth."

"Here, try this," Jazzy said, pulling another dress off the pile of outfits stacked in the fitting room. "One is bound to work."

She zipped me into a tight red spaghetti-strapped number. "We've hit a home run, Trix!" Jazzy exclaimed.

I looked at myself in the fabulous dress. We posed side by side.

"Who'd ever have thought, Trix, that two bush girls would wind up with super-hot dates to the prom."

"I still can't believe it. I remember you and me sitting in study hall staring at Gavin and Stinkface."

"In two weeks we'll be snuggling close with our men in front of the whole school. And then after the prom we'll have them all to ourselves. Ricky rented a hotel room and everything."

"The only hotels I can stay at are ones used on family vacations."

"Trix, it's the prom. It's Gavin Baldwin."

"Sarge wouldn't let me stay at a hotel with the pope!"

"You can always stop by for a visit," she said, raising an eyebrow.

"If you want my mother to show up too . . . oh, Jazz, I just can't believe it. Me and Gavin Baldwin, walking into senior prom together. Me and him and a corsage!"

"It is so flash!" she said, squeezing my hand. "Our dreams are coming true!"

"And by the looks of it," I said, glancing at the price tag, "dreams can be really expensive."

Friday night at Chaplin's. With much begging, Vic let me feature through the weekend. Dad even let me drive myself home, since the White Sox were on TV.

"I loathe high school," I began. An unassuming stout man opened the theater door. He stood in the back and glanced around the club. Audience and staff around him were distracted by his presence, whispering and staring at him. He finally took a seat with Vic at a back table, hidden in the shadows.

"Make sure he has a doctor's excuse for arriving late," I commented to the audience. "I guess he had to buy scalped tickets."

Since it wasn't Gavin, his entrance didn't derail my routine. I returned to my material and finished without a hitch. When I came off the stage, Vic's friend was gone.

"Trixie," Vic said emphatically, waving me over. "We have a guest tonight. He wants to try out some new material. You'll have to introduce him after Chuck finishes."

"I have to memorize another name?" I whined.

"I think you'll remember this one. It's Jelly Bean."

"Jelly Bean? You mean *the* Jelly Bean? The comedian? Yeah, right. And I play center for the Bulls!"

Just then the theater doors cracked open into the lobby, and I could see a man in a maroon jogging suit surrounded by a small gathering, towering over a college cutie—signing an autograph.

My eyes lit up. Jelly Bean? Here? This couldn't be true! Touring professionals came in and out of Chaplin's every week—Vic told stories about celebrities showing up, but I thought they were just stories. Since I'd been working Chaplin's, the only celebrity I had seen was Tony Danza—and he was in the audience. But Jelly Bean? I was in the presence of greatness!

"No way!" I begged Vic. "When did he come in? Oh no!" I exclaimed with sudden revelation. He was the man who came in late! I told the audience Jelly Bean bought scalped tickets!

"Have a nervous breakdown after the show," Vic said,

stubbing out his cigarette in an ashtray.

I buried myself at a side table. I wanted to ask Jelly for his autograph, yet I wanted to behave like a professional. But the reality was that I was a total mess. I wanted to giggle, cry, scream, and bow down at his feet all at the same time. I wanted to call Sarge, Jazzy, Gavin, but there wasn't enough time. Chuck was cutting his set short, so I had to pay close attention for the introduction cue.

"Thank you very much," Chuck said to the audience, and hopped offstage.

I sucked a straw like it was a cigarette and ran from my lookout post to fill the empty stage. "We have a special guest tonight here at Chaplin's. A comedy legend, a major movie star, and a framed poster on my wall! Give a big hand for Jelly Bean!"

Jelly Bean sauntered onstage with a cigar to thunderous applause. His huge hand swallowed my tiny hand. I stood frozen, staring up at the massive megastar.

"I can't believe you're standing here," I proclaimed like a gushy groupie.

"I can't believe it either, not after eating three Chaplin burgers."

The crowd went wild. I realized I was still onstage and quickly hurried off, grabbing an empty seat at a front table.

"People say TV adds ten pounds," he began, standing

massively in his brightly colored sweat suit. "You can see I've been on TV a lot. I better get a radio job before I explode!" he said wildly, taking a puff from his cigar as we laughed.

"Don't tell me I'm not charitable. I've made donations to a starving third world country. I've been donating fat!"

I had never heard a reaction like this before. Everyone laughed hysterically and sat glued to his every word. Out of all the comics I'd ever watched live, none held the audience in the palm of his hands like Jelly. He was a master. He could have blown his nose and gotten a standing ovation. My cheeks hurt from laughing so hard.

After his set, he was whisked away by Vic while I made final announcements. I ran offstage but Jelly Bean had gone. Where did he go? Maybe he was staying at the Amber Hills Hotel or the Four Seasons—locked inside a celebrity suite. My one glimpse of my hero and no photograph, no signature, no proof of his presence.

I ran to the lobby to use my cell phone—one of the perks of making two hundred dollars a week—and called Jazzy. I was dramatically recounting my incredible tale when Vic called me back into the club.

"I want you to meet someone."

I followed Vic to his empty table. Just then Jelly Bean stepped out from the kitchen, carrying a basket of chicken wings.

I was in the presence of a legend. My framed poster was coming alive and walking toward me.

"Jelly Bean, this is Trixie Shapiro."

"I worship you! I totally love you!" I blubbered uncontrollably.

"We were just talking about you," Jelly Bean said with a smile. "Sit down, please."

"I've got all your CDs!" I rambled on. "I own your HBO special—*Jelly Bean Live and Artificially Flavored*, and *Jelly Bean—The Movie*."

"Sit down—please!" he insisted as he scooted himself into a seat.

"Thanks," I said, plopping into a chair. "I'd hate to faint in front of you."

"What are you drinking?" he asked.

"Anything you want me to," I exclaimed.

Jelly Bean flagged the waitress and ordered me a Coke.

"Chicken wing?" he asked, handing me the basket.

I'd eat a squirrel soaked in cheese if it came from Jelly Bean.

I laid the wing on a cocktail napkin and pulled off a tiny piece of meat, afraid sauce would smear on my face.

"So how long have you been doing stand-up?" Jelly Bean asked.

"Since the beginning of the school year."

"Man," Jelly Bean said, turning his attention to Vic. "Do you remember when time was measured in school years? A year lasted nine months. An hour lasted fifty-five minutes. Now I measure a year by my annual prostate exam."

"Jelly Bean has a job for you," Vic said.

"You want me to baby-sit your kids?"

"I'm doing Vegas in two weeks," Jelly Bean began. "My opener is going to be out for two nights and I want you to emcee."

I thought I was hearing things. "Me? You want me?"

"Would you rather suggest someone else?"

"But you can get anyone—you're Jelly Bean!"

"I want a woman, and someone whose act is completely different from mine. No jokes about overeating, marriage, or growing up in the South. And I want someone who's totally clean. You're a girl, you're in high school, and you handle yourself well onstage—except when I'm standing next to you. We'll have to rehearse that part," he joked.

My mouth dangled in disbelief.

"Who's your manager?" he continued.

"Manager?" I asked.

"Who runs your career?" he asked, tearing into another wing.

190

"My mother runs my life! Does that count?"

"My agent will call you to confirm the dates and make your travel arrangements."

"But what if I bomb?" I asked nervously.

"The worse you are, the better I look!" he said with a wink.

But Jelly Bean, of course, was kidding. I'd have to be excellent—he'd want the entire show to kill.

I used my cell phone and called Sid from the bathroom stall in Chaplin's.

"What's up, Shrimp?" he shouted, the Rolling Stones blaring in the background.

"I just met Jelly Bean!"

"Who?"

"Jelly Bean!" I yelled.

"Kill the tunes, dude. My sister's calling," he hollered. Mick Jagger was suddenly silenced.

"Jelly Bean?" he asked. "No way!"

"Yes way! And he wants me to open for him in Vegas!"

"You rock, sista!"

"But I have a dilemma," I confessed.

"You need to get out of another Talent Night?" he asked.

"No, the prom."

"You mean Gavin asked you?"

"He did," I said, with a warm glow I knew he felt through the phone.

"Congrats! Why don't you want to go?"

"Vegas is the same time as the prom," I whined.

"Didn't this happen to you before at the Veins concert?"

"Yes, but I was just around the corner from the club."

"Then blow off the prom."

"And Gavin?"

"Invite him," he advised. "Like *anyone* would rather go to Vegas than the prom."

"This is Sin City. I'm not playing in the Hamptons. Gavin comes from a prominent family. I don't think anyone on his family tree ever missed a prom."

"I think Sarge is the bigger issue. She's not going to let you go alone to Vegas with Gavin."

"Would you take me? I mean us?"

"That would rule, girl. But I blew this month's rent on a Phish concert last weekend. And why are you calling me from Chaplin's?"

"I needed to talk to you before I talked to Sarge. What do I do?"

"Ask Gavin to go with you. He'll be the coolest senior in Vegas."

"And Sarge?"

"She'll be the uncoolest senior," he said, and hung up.

I screamed in the car the whole two blocks to my house. Excited and petrified, I burst open our front door and found my parents on the sofa, Sarge sleeping and Dad watching TV.

"You'll never believe it! Jelly Bean was at the club! He saw my act and he wants me to emcee two of his shows in Vegas."

My parents were stunned and didn't say a word.

"Slow down," my father finally said.

"I'm not kidding. Jelly Bean—wants me to emcee for him in Vegas!"

"Congratulations!" my dad exclaimed, getting up and hugging me.

"Let me in!" Sarge said, running to me. "I want to hug the star!"

"He liked your show?" Dad asked excitedly.

"Apparently he loved her show!" Sarge exclaimed proudly. "Does this mean you'll invite him over for dinner?"

"He's not coming to dinner! We're going to Vegas!" I yelled, dancing around. "Me! Little Trixie Shapiro will be opening for the massively huge—and I'm not talking about his physique—Jelly Bean!"

"My girl is going to be a Las Vegas emcee showgirl," Sarge said, hugging me again.

"I'm just afraid this is all a dream," I said.

"If it was a dream you'll find your room neat as a pin," Sarge teased.

"No, that's your dream!" I said, laughing.

"So when's the show?" Dad finally asked.

"In two weeks! I'll have to miss at least one day of school."

"School?" Sarge asked, changing her tone.

"School, schmool!"

"Your grades are slipping down the alphabet. I'm very happy for you, Trixie, but since your SAT scores were low, your time in school is very important."

"I'll study in Vegas!"

"I don't know. . . ," Sarge said, hesitantly.

"She'll study in Vegas," Dad said in my defense.

"And I'll miss the prom too," I said. "It's on the same weekend."

"Do we have to write you an excuse for that too?" Dad joked.

"Prom? But Gavin will be so disappointed. And you already bought your dress!" Sarge reminded me.

"I know, but millions of girls don't go to their prom and they end up with jobs and families and lives."

"Just a dance?" Sarge repeated.

"I know . . . what if I invited him?" I asked.

"To Vegas? It's not exactly an acceptable field trip,

Trixie. And let's get back to the school discussion—how do we explain this to your teacher?" Sarge worried.

"I'll get Jelly Bean to write me an excuse."

Dad changed the subject.

"You're not going to change your name, are you? You'll keep 'Shapiro,' won't you?" my dad asked.

"Of course!"

"I don't mind if you change 'Trixie.'"

"But she was named for my aunt Tiffany!" my mother said.

"Trixie Shapiro has a nice sound to it," my father said dreamily.

"I'm not changing my name, people!"

"My little girl, I'm so proud of you," Dad said, hugging me.

"Congratulations!" my mom screamed, throwing her arms around us.

I smiled a huge smile as I was sandwiched between them.

"I have an in-service that Friday!" Sarge complained. "I'll have to take a late flight!"

"I can go to Vegas and meet you guys there," I offered. "I'm too old to have a stage mother."

"But you're not to old to have a stage father," Dad declared.

"You thought we'd let you go to Vegas with Gavin

unchaperoned?" Sarge asked.

"No. Then I'd really know this was all a dream."

I news-flashed Jazzy first thing the next morning and then raced over to Gavin's house.

"I have awesome news!" Gavin exclaimed, opening his bedroom door.

"Me too!" I exclaimed.

"You've also been accepted?" he asked. "Congratulations! This is totally amazing! Maybe sophomore year I can get an apartment and we can meet in my swinging pad between classes!"

"Accepted? Uh . . . Congrats! I just—"

He pulled me onto his bed and kissed me longingly. "I love you," he said.

Wait! Stop everything! Jelly Bean has just booked me for Las Vegas, and now Gavin Baldwin—the Gavin Baldwin—has said he loves me! Was I in the Twilight Zone?

"What did you just say?" I asked, pulling him up, straddling his lap.

"Well—," he said, pulling at a thread on his bedspread.

"Yes?" I asked, turning his face toward mine.

"I already said it!"

"But tell me again!" I exclaimed, tugging at the collar

of his shirt. "I want to make sure I heard you correctly."

"You heard me!"

"I didn't hear you!" I said.

"I love you," he whispered in my ear.

"I didn't hear you in this ear," I said, smiling, turning my head.

"Come on already!"

"I totally love you too. But I've always loved you."

I'd never said that to Gavin. In my thoughts, in my dreams. But it fell out of my mouth as naturally as if I'd said it to his face a thousand times.

"I want us to celebrate, before my parents come home," he said, running his fingers underneath the back of my shirt.

"Do you have champagne?" I asked.

"No, but I have something else," he said, leaning back and pulling me with him.

"Gavin!" I said, giggling like crazy as he tickled my belly.

And for the afternoon, I forgot all about the senior prom, Vegas, and a star named Jelly Bean.

"Before you know it, you'll have your own sitcom," Jazzy screamed at the Sunrise Coffee Shop at dinner-time. "Can I be the nosy neighbor? Please, please!"

"Chill! I'm just emceeing. People aren't coming to Vegas to see me."

"But they will! This month you'll be hanging with the Jelly Man. Next month you'll be on the *Douglas Douglas Show*. A mansion in L.A. for you and your true-blue best friend is so happening right now. I just can't believe it's the same night as the prom! What did Gavin say?"

"He said he loved me."

"After you told him about Vegas?"

"No, like right after he told me about Northwestern. He doesn't know about Vegas."

"He doesn't know about Vegas?"

"I wanted to tell him. But he was so excited—I mean, happy!"

"Man. Vegas is way farther than the Mosh Pit. How can you be two places at once this time? You'll need the Concorde!"

I laughed.

"Don't worry, I can think of something. But, really, who needs the prom when you can be hanging out with Adam Sandler and Ben Stiller. Don't get me wrong, I think Gavin is hot, but when it comes down to it, how many films has he starred in?" said Jazzy.

"Jazz! I've been in love with him for over two years and today he said he loved me. I'd do anything for him. Besides, I already have a plan. I'm going to ask Gavin to go with me."

"But I thought I was the one with the plans. Don't outgrow me."

"Is that possible?"

"Yeah, I guess you're right. I'm pretty stellar!" she said, laughing. "This is so cool! Vegas is Sin City! They have Jacuzzis in the rooms! And people that perform marriages twenty-four hours a day. You could come back married."

"Thanks for the support. Even though I'm ecstatic about Vegas, I still wish this wasn't happening on prom weekend. I'll miss you, the dance of a lifetime, and our double dream dates."

"You get to go to Vegas! What more do you want?"

"For Jelly Bean to host our prom."

THE INVITATION

☆

This time I wasn't going to let Gavin distract me. I packed a picnic lunch complete with tiny cheeses, crackers, and sparkling grape juice. I hoped he wouldn't be too disappointed about the prom, because this was a killer opportunity for us both. The two of us sharing Vegas, meeting Jelly Bean.

I was flying my two-dollar kite high over Lake Michigan while Gavin lay on the rocks. The weather was perfect, the water splashing up against the rocks, the lake filled with billowing sailboats.

"I should have gotten a plastic handle," I wailed, trying to control the kite.

"Calm down," he said, tying the string to the picnic basket. "Picnics are supposed to be relaxing."

"I'm just excited! I have something to ask you and I'm bursting!" I exclaimed, sitting next to him on the rocks. "I wanted to ask you yesterday, but you distracted me—"

"I believe there was mutual distracting going on," he said.

"Gavin!" I said, pulling away. "I'll never get to ask you if you keep doing that."

"Okay," he said, reluctantly sitting up. "So what's up?"

"Friday at Chaplin's . . . who shows up at the beginning of my set but, none other than—Jelly Bean!"

"You're kidding! Jelly Bean? I'd kill to see him! How long was he there? Why didn't you call me?"

"Well, that's what I want to ask you about," I answered.

"*He* wouldn't get nervous if I watched," he teased.

"Shhh!" I said, placing my finger over his lips. "After the show, Jelly Bean asked me to fill in for his emcee for two shows in Vegas. . . . Unfortunately it's the same weekend as the prom. So I'm asking you to come with me to Vegas!"

Gavin wasn't screaming like Jazzy did. He wasn't jumping like Sarge and Dad. It was almost as if he didn't understand.

"Well?" I asked excitedly. "A lot to swallow, right?"

"Wow—," he said, with shocked eyes. "That's . . . way cool," he said, with a smile that almost seemed forced.

"Unbelievable, really," I said, grabbing his hand. "I still think I'm dreaming! Can you believe that something like this would happen to me—to us!"

"Wow, Trix. This is great," he said, squeezing my hand. "Congratulations."

I expected a kiss or a hug—not a hand squeeze.

"So you'll be emceeing like you do at Chaplin's?" he asked. "Where you'll introduce him and I'll have to stand in the hallway?"

"No! I want you there. In the back—but I want you there."

Gavin fingered the kite's string as it soared higher in the sky.

"But this is Vegas, Trix, not Chaplin's. So now you'll be traveling the country with Jelly Bean?" he asked, trying to process the info.

"No, silly! It's two nights only."

"Two nights now—six weeks when you arrive. Trixie, this is major! You have no idea where this could lead. He could introduce you to stars. He could take you to L.A."

"Jelly Bean? He can take me wherever he wants, baby!" I said, with a laugh. "But seriously, I'm lucky if he doesn't fire me because I'll be shaking so badly!"

"I don't know about this . . . ," Gavin said, playing with the kite string. "Vegas isn't Chaplin's, Trix. The guys that go there—they have money, smoke fat cigars, they can spot seventeen-year-old girls like a hunter spots a fox."

"You sound like my mother! Besides, you can be my bodyguard."

Gavin scratched his neck distractedly. "I guess I just expected we'd go to the prom."

"I know. I've waited for the prom for all my life. But

Vegas—Jazzy says they have Jacuzzis in the rooms and waterfalls in the pools!"

"We'll be sharing a room?" he asked, surprised.

"Well, actually you'll be sharing a room with my dad."

I turned to my kite, which began circling out of control in the wind.

"So you'll go?" I asked.

Gavin stared up at the kite. "I'll have to think about it," he said.

"What's there to think about?"

"I already paid for tickets to the prom, my tux, and the deposit on the limo. I know Vegas is once in a lifetime . . . but . . . , " he began.

"But what?"

"I want to go to the prom," he said, standing up.

"I want to go too!" I said, following him.

"No. I mean I'm *going* to the prom," he said strongly. "And I want you to go too."

I didn't know what to say. "I'm confused."

"I invited you first. You already said yes to me."

"What's happening, Gavin?"

Love seemed to rush out of him while terror filled me.

"It's not about the prom. Don't you see? It's about us," he contested.

"If I give this opportunity up," I argued, "it could cost me my career."

"You could pursue it later. What about North-western?"

"You sound like Sarge. I'd never ask you to give up being an architect. Guys never give up their careers for girls. Is this what you really want me to do, Gavin?"

"You have to make a decision," he said firmly. "Jazzy isn't here to sign you up for Talent Night. Janson isn't here to force you to do Open Mike. Ben's not pushing you into an amateur contest, or Jelly Bean and Las Vegas. And Sergeant isn't here to tell you to give up all your current success for college. It's your life. And you have to grow up and decide how the hell you want to live it."

I was stunned. I'd never seen Gavin so forceful. I couldn't believe what he was asking me.

"You're asking me to choose?" I cried.

My dreams were turning upside down.

"I guess I am," he said quietly.

"You are!" I shouted. "You're asking me to give up comedy! How can I make a choice?"

He stared at me, waiting for my reply.

"We're talking about my soul, Gavin. This is all I've ever wanted."

"Are you talking about me . . . or comedy?" he asked, confused.

"Both—I'm talking about my life. I don't have time to daydream anymore. For the first time in my life, I feel alive! Life is happening to me. Don't you see that?"

"What do you want, Trixie?" he asked, frustrated.

"I want you!" I said, hugging him, tears streaming down my face. I could feel his soft cotton shirt bunch up in my hands, my fingertips touching his warm back. I couldn't let go. "For two years I've watched you walk down the halls, envied the lockers you leaned against. I knew that you ate turkey sandwiches for lunch, that you smelled of Obsession as you sauntered by. And now I know how you kiss, touch, feel. . . . How could I choose anything but you?"

And I remembered my first laugh in my living room, and how much I'd accomplished since that moment.

He caressed my hair and kissed the top of my head. I looked up at him, his dreamy lips, his sparkling blue eyes, and I said, "But I'm going to Vegas."

The words hit him like a bolt of lightning. The girl he held in his arms had made a choice. The choice wasn't him.

Gavin backed away. Rage burned in his eyes.

He picked up his backpack and slung it over his shoulder.

"Gavin . . . please —"

"Send me a postcard," he called in a huff as he walked away.

"I already know what it'll say," I called, tears flooding my eyes. "Wish you were here. . . ."

HEADLINING

VIVA LAS VEGAS

☆

"I had no idea the prom was so important to him," I cried to Jazzy as I sat on my bed, puffy-eyed. "He's attended the prom since he was a freshman. Seniors were always asking him. I'll be standing onstage with Jelly Bean for two seconds. Gavin will be holding a girl in his arms for hours. I can't even bear the thought. He can't go with Stinkface! You have to set him up with . . . your mother—she's beautiful!"

"You're hearing just prom—Gavin's hearing he's not important anymore," Jazzy speculated.

"But he is!"

"The prom is the biggest night of a teenager's life," Jazzy continued. "For bush girls to go is a dream come true—much less to be going with hipsters. But Gavin is a coolhead—his destiny wasn't to be taking tickets at the door. He could possibly be crowned Prom Stud."

"I thought you said this wasn't about the prom!"

"Everything's changed! The biggest day of your life now far outshines the biggest day of his life. The relationship was about you worshipping Gavin. Now Gavin has to worship you. He can be the big fish of Mason, but maybe he can't be Gavin Shapiro."

"I'm not asking him to be."

"Girl, he just realized you've outgrown him!"

Jazzy's assessment of the situation wasn't reaching me. "But I'm still a bush girl! I still love Gavin, whether I'm standing on a stage in Vegas or dancing under a disco ball at Mason High. Why can't he understand that? Why can't he understand that an opportunity like this only happens once?"

"He does, Trixie! That's why he's freaking out. I've been going to therapy long enough to see the situation. He's afraid of your success. He's afraid of losing you."

"Well, he did lose me—and I lost him."

"You have to forget him—you're on a rising rocket to fame! You meet comics all the time—there'll be hundreds of lonely guys just waiting to date you."

"But not one named Gavin Baldwin."

"Well, you can sit on this bed and cry forever, or you can go to Vegas and rock the world."

I thought for a moment.

"You're right. You're right!" I said apologetically. "I guess I've made a decision—just like Gavin demanded."

The show must go on.

★ ★ ★

My eyes were already haggard from performing at Chaplin's and school. Now they were puffy and swollen from crying. I couldn't turn my love for Gavin off like some amorous light switch. I buried myself in rehearsing and writing new jokes for Jelly Bean's show. I used cucumber eye presses, extra rouge, and Joyful aromatherapy spray to mask my exterior, but nothing could hide or truly distract me from the hole I felt inside.

When I closed my comedy notebook or stepped off the stage at Chaplin's, I was sadder than I had ever been in my life. I felt more unappreciated than I had before ever knowing an audience's approval, lonelier than before I received my first smile from Gavin.

Gavin didn't call and beg for my return. He didn't say he missed me. He didn't smile when we passed in the halls. Now I was counting his frowns.

And I was supposed to think about Vegas. My offstage life had become desperate, torturous, endless. Each night as I slept in my Varicose Veins T-shirt, I asked myself if I'd made the right choice. Why did I want this crazy life anyway? Cam was lonely and miserable—and he was successful. Did I want to live the rest of my life out of a suitcase, eating meals from a vending machine, only to return home from the road to a moldy refrigerator and an empty bed?

★ ★ ★

The next week Sarge waited with us at the gate before Dad and I boarded the plane, as if I was a ten-year-old child. I was getting motion sickness from Sarge squeezing her "little baby" back and forth.

As I buckled myself into my window seat, I caught a glimpse of my reflection in the window. Unbelievable. Trixie Shapiro was heading to Vegas!

Millions of lights illuminated a neon paradise as the plane swept over the Strip. Mandalay Bay, the Luxor, Excalibur, the MGM Grand all flickered their welcome.

It looked like the airplane had landed right in the middle of a circus. I was truly in Casino Country. Gamblers didn't have to go farther than the airport gate with hopes of winning millions. Flashing neon lights, the *ching ching* of spinning slot machines were within sight of the departure and arrival gates. Huge video screens advertised shows as bags spun around on the conveyer belts.

Dad and I were greeted by a silver-haired man in a dark suit, holding a white sign that read: TRIXIE SHAPERO.

"You are going to be famous," my dad said. "Look, they are already misspelling your name."

I only felt the desert heat for the two minutes it took to follow my driver—yes, my driver!—from the air-conditioned terminal to his air-conditioned Ford

Explorer. Unlike Chicago, where it can take all weekend to get from O'Hare to the city, Las Vegas has its airport literally blocks from the Strip—mega blocks large enough to hold enormous hotels and their supercolossal signs, an Eiffel Tower, a pirate ship, a pyramid, a castle with a wizard, and Roman columns.

We pulled into the circular drive of our hotel—Legends. Before us rose the facade of a massive 1940s-style movie theater that housed twelve movie theaters inside—as well as the obligatory casino, three thousand rooms, swimming pools, restaurants, and an empty stage where I was to make my Vegas debut.

The driver handed the valet our bags and said to my dad, "Win a million, Mr. Shapiro."

"What are you doing?" I asked my dad. His head was tilted back as he craned his neck to see the marquis.

"I wanted to see if your name is in lights."

But all it read was "Jelly Bean Live."

The Legends' huge oak doors automatically opened, revealing a moving sidewalk in a dark corridor. As soon as we stepped on it, lights flashed and camera shutters clicked, simulating a hundred paparazzi. Invisible fans "oohed" and "aahed" and shouted, "Look this way," and "Can I have your autograph?"

We were swept into a bright, cavernous lobby. Long rows of check-in desks were designed like old-fashioned ticket windows.

"Trixie Shapiro," I announced as Dad sat next to a lobby poster of *Rebel Without a Cause*. Sarge had always been the one to check the family into hotels, and now Dad was letting me take charge. I felt a surge of self-confidence at finally getting the opportunity to take care of myself.

"Welcome to Vegas," the woman said through the window. "Your name again?

"Shapiro."

She pressed the keyboard on her computer. "We don't have a reservation. Could it be under another name?"

"How about S-h-a-p-e-r-o."

She fiddled with the keys. "I'm sorry, no listing."

Impossible. Did I have the wrong hotel? Did I have the wrong week?

"This is Legends, isn't it?" I asked, suddenly confused.

"Yes."

"Jelly Bean is performing here tonight, isn't he?"

"Yes, he is."

This was exactly the kind of thing Cam had talked about. Life on the road!

"Are you here with your parents?" she asked skeptically.

"No, I'm here with Jelly Bean. I'm opening for him tonight, and I need rest."

"Hold on," she said, suddenly polite, and tapped her

fingers again. "We're crowded this weekend because of a Barbie Doll convention. Let me see . . . I can put you in room four fifteen."

"Thanks. But I'll need two rooms, please." She looked at me strangely. "My entourage," I explained, pointing to my father.

"You're in luck. Four seventeen is available too."

"What kind of luck is that?"

The casino was magnificent. A huge movie screen showed Laurel and Hardy tripping on a banana, but the slot addicts only had eyes for apples, oranges, and lemons. At the blackjack tables, dealers were dressed in usher outfits, and Marilyn Monroes, James Deans, and Groucho Marxes pushed money-changing carts.

Dad and I were lost. We circled the Walk of Fame three times before Humphrey Bogart pointed us to the elevators.

A golden star with room number 415 greeted me. I stuck my key card inside the door slot and got the green light. My very own Vegas bedroom. What awaited me on the other side? A pink neon headboard? Glittery bathrobes? A roulette wheel Jacuzzi? A slot machine toilet handle that ching-chinged with every flush?

But it was like any other hotel room—except for framed pictures of Marlon Brando, W.C. Fields, and Mae West adorning the walls. After all, management didn't want travelers wasting time on roulette wheel Jacuzzis when they could be losing money at the real thing. I waved Dad good-bye and, after he disappeared through the adjoining door, I immediately called Jazzy with his phone card.

"I have my very own room in Vegas!" I shouted. "I can bounce on the beds and there's no Sarge to yell at me. Only housekeeping!"

I was too wired to rest and opened the curtains. The neon lights glistened from the surrounding hotels, but in the distance lay vast desert and darkness. I felt its loneliness and was overcome with thoughts of Gavin. My stomach sank as I caught my somber reflection in the dark glass.

I rode the elevator back to the lobby to find my way to the Living Legends Comedy Club, not to be confused with their twenty-thousand-seat concert hall. I thought I had stumbled upon the ladies' room, but it was indeed the club's entrance. A poster of Jelly Bean hung on the wall.

I pulled the doors open and peeked in.

I expected Carnegie Hall, but this was more like Chaplin's on a good night. It held about two hundred people, with round tables and chairs and little unlit candles on the tables. The stage looked about the same size as my hotel bed.

A man dressed in tech black walked in. "May I help you?" he asked.

"I'm Trixie Shapiro," I said, extending my hand. "I'm opening for Jelly Bean tonight."

"I'm Kevin," he said, shaking my hand. "I'm glad you're here. I need to test the lighting levels."

I jumped up onstage and looked at the empty chairs. In a few hours they would be filled. Stage fright set in. My stomach turned. This wouldn't be an Amber Hills audience.

"Where's Jelly Bean?" I asked as he walked back up to the lighting booth.

"You'll be lucky if you get to see him before he goes on. He usually secludes himself in his dressing room until he's announced."

Good, maybe then he won't know if I bomb.

Kevin brought up the stage lights.

Then he hit the follow spot. I saw dust flying from the stage. I felt the warm glow from the Vegas spotlight.

I had arrived.

Two hours later a line formed outside the theater, reaching the casino bar. I hung out with Ray, the bartender. He passed a vodka to a businessman. I wanted to intercept the pass and liquify my nerves, but I never drank anything stronger than wine at Passover seder, and that always sent me into a giggling frenzy. That's all I needed—to laugh at my own jokes while the audience sat quietly.

I took my Coke without ice back to the dressing room as more audience members arrived, waiting for the theater doors to open.

I gazed into the mirror, fixing my hair and makeup. In a few minutes I'd be playing Vegas. But instead of seeing "Trixie Shapiro, rising Las Vegas star," I saw an insecure senior at Mason High who was missing her prom.

"Ready, Trixie?" asked Sandy, the stage manager, knocking on my door.

"No!" I called back with a quiver in my voice. "But that won't stop me."

I could hear Kevin on the loudspeaker. "Tonight, Legends Hotel proudly presents live and in person, a true comic legend himself, Jelly Bean! But before we bring him out, we have a special guest to start you laughing, straight from Chicago—Trixie Shapiro!"

The audience applauded politely as I walked out onto a real Las Vegas stage. I picked up the microphone, gazed at the packed house, and panicked. The youngest person in the audience was at least thirty years old. I prayed they would remember how it felt to be in high school and took a deep breath. My mouth was sans saliva and it was impossible to swallow.

"Vegas is really for adults. I was the only kid on the airplane. I had to use my fake ID just to get peanuts!"

The audience laughed. I gulped air.

"And this town is totally obsessed with gambling. My hotel room is crazy. The back of the toilet is set up like a slot machine. The only way to flush the toilet is to pull the lever and get three lemons."

I looked around at the audience of smiling and laughing faces. "Legends just built a kiddie casino. I spent all my milk money. And wiped out my college fund!

"I loathe high school. I'm unbearably shy, afraid to speak up in class. I'm not the class clown—I'm the class mime!"

I had feared my fifteen minutes of fame would seem like fifteen years, but before I knew it I was saying, "Thank you, and now the man you have all been waiting for—the fabulous Jelly Bean!"

I watched Jelly Bean's brilliant performance from backstage. He closed the show himself. Afterward he secluded himself in his dressing room while I sat wired, washing my face in my dressing-room sink. Jelly Bean wouldn't receive visitors—or eager young comediennes—until after both shows were over.

The audience gave me a standing ovation as I finished my
set. I ran offstage and bumped into a bright bouquet of roses.
"You were terrific!" Gavin exclaimed.
"But you're supposed to be at the prom!" I said, surprised.
"No," he corrected, kissing me. "I'm supposed to be with
you."

Jet lag kicked in during my second set, and my monologue wasn't as punchy. The audience took an eternity to
laugh.

I finished my last joke to courteous applause and sat in
the wings sleepy-eyed while Jelly Bean won over the
audience with a comical wizard's spell.

Afterward I waited in my dressing room while Jelly
received fans, friends, and family. I hoped to speak to
him for a minute and find out if he heard any of my performance, but he and his wife rushed past my door with
a generic "Good night, everyone!"

I might have been exhausted, but I was also starving.
Dad took me to the buffet and I ate like a linebacker. I'd
never seen my dad glow so much. Maybe it was the fluorescent lighting. When we finally returned upstairs, it
was almost dawn Chicago time, too late to call Jazzy, and
too early to call Sarge. No time was the right time for
Gavin anymore. But I couldn't complain. As I collapsed

on my bed, still fully dressed, I could only wonder what one dreams of once a dream comes true.

After a few hours of restless sleep and a light breakfast, Dad and I sat poolside, trying to relax before Sergeant showed up. She arrived in time for lunch in full loudness—there was a deafening banging coming from the adjoining room that sounded like the TV had fallen on Dad. I opened the adjoining door, and there was Sarge, yelling, "I'm here! We'll leave the doors wide open so I can see you better!"

I had a feeling I'd be sleeping in the bathtub.

Sergeant hadn't seen me perform since she'd snuck into Chaplin's.

But now that I knew Sarge was in the house, my fear of stage fright was compounded by the terror that she'd grab the microphone.

But it was too late. Instead of Kevin's voice over the loudspeaker, a familiar woman's loud voice, complete with a Chicago accent, began the introduction to the show. Not Sarge! "She came into the world crying," she began, "and spent the rest of her life laughing. You've seen her as a naked baby in a bathtub on America's Most Embarrassing Videos . . . Ladies and gentleman, from dirty diapers to dirty jokes, my little baby girl, Trixie Shapiro."

I walked up on stage and stood frozen. The audience was already laughing, but not with me—at me.

"Don't blow this!" was all I could think when Kevin announced my name. I had my material safely tucked in my bra just in case I blanked out. Hopefully I wouldn't forget where I put the note.

I couldn't see my parents anywhere with the stage light blinding my view of the back table.

I took a deep breath and began, "My mother flew in to Vegas tonight. She plans to open her own hotel. It's called Sergeant's. Guests have a curfew, and if they are not back in their hotel rooms by eleven they are grounded! Mom is a professional nag—she mastered in Yelling with a Ph.D. in Whining."

I could hear Sergeant's cackling from the back of the room as I plugged away at my punch lines. At first I found it distracting, then comforting, like a comical umbilical cord.

After all, if Sarge could laugh at herself, then maybe I could take myself less seriously.

"My little baby!" she exclaimed, barging into my small dressing room after the show. "You were wonderful!" she continued. Dad followed, carrying a bouquet of flowers.

Just then Jelly Bean walked by.

"Thank you for helping our Trixie," my mother hollered, racing over to him.

He turned away and hurried into his dressing room.

"Mom! You can't talk to him between shows," I said, pulling her back into my room.

"What do you mean I can't talk to him? I just listened to him talk for an hour! The least he can do is listen to me for five minutes!"

"Ma!" I said through clenched teeth.

"You were great, once again!" Dad said, handing me the flowers.

"You think so?"

"Yes!" Sarge gushed. "You were fantastic!" She hugged me with all her might.

"Sensational!" Dad said.

"You looked beautiful up there. But the lights wash you out. You need foundation," Sarge said, rummaging in her purse.

"So what did you really think?" I asked my dad.

"What's there to think? It was perfect."

The stage manager tapped on the door. "We start in fifteen."

"I need to veg, okay?" I told my parents.

"You sure you can't get us a closer table?" Sarge asked.

"You're close enough."

"I know you're embarrassed having your mother around. . . ," Sarge began.

"We'll see you after the show," my dad said, leading Sarge out.

"Thanks for coming, Mom," I called after her.

I felt exhilarated. I had climbed several rungs of life's ladder tonight and I was pumped for the second show. I was pacing in the hallway when an intense-looking man wearing a million-dollar black suit left Jelly Bean's dressing room.

Jelly never received guests before the show. This man had to be important. Maybe threatening. Was he with the mob? After all, this was Vegas.

The mobster did a double take when he saw me. He slowly approached, with an extreme seriousness that made me want to call for Elliot Ness. My overimaginative heart raced when he reached into his breast pocket. He pulled out a business card and said, "We'll call."

I felt faint. Mobsters Inc. We protect—you pay.

Maybe they owned Legends. Maybe they extorted comedians. Maybe they extorted the audience. Had I said anything in my act that might have offended him?

I searched my memory as I turned over the card:

Derek Jacobson
Booker
The *Douglas Douglas Show*

I almost fainted.

I'd hit the jackpot!

I was gathering my flowers, Sarge's foundation, my bottled water, and my precious business card after the second show when I heard a knock on my dressing-room door.

"You've got a visitor," Sandy said, peeking in. "It's a guy, with luscious black hair. And boy is he cute!"

Gavin? I quickly fluffed my hair and re-applied ruby-red lipstick. He had skipped the prom after all to meet me in Vegas.

Gavin stood in the dressing-room doorway, his Carribean ocean eyes staring through me. "I've missed you, Starbaby. I couldn't go to the prom without you. So I came here."

"Hey, sweetheart!" my black-haired visitor shouted, pulling me back into reality.

"Sid! No way! I can't believe you're here!" My eyes welled up with tears. Although I was disappointed Gavin hadn't forsaken the prom for me after all, I was over-whelmed to see my brother.

"I caught most of the second show. That bit about Sarge teaching classes to the hotel maids was killer!"

"Speak of the devil," Sarge said, bursting in with Dad at her side.

"You were awesome. Did you tell Jelly Bean I discovered you?" Sid teased. "I knew you would be a star, even then."

I glowed from my brother's compliments. I'd never heard him speak like this.

I heard Jelly Bean pass down the hall. "Quick, guys!" I said, grabbing my brother's arm.

"Jelly Bean," I called. "Do you have a sec?"

"For you, I even have half a minute," Jelly Bean said.

"Jelly Bean, this is my big brother, Sid."

I hung back as Sid stood starstruck next to the massive Jelly. I hadn't seen Sid smile like that since we played football in the basement and he scored a touchdown.

"And I'm her mother!" Sarge burst forth. "Thank you for giving her this wonderful opportunity."

"Shh, Ma!" I whispered harshly.

"It's my pleasure," Jelly said.

"I've worried so, comedy being filled with filthy language and all. I didn't want my daughter—"

"I wouldn't want my daughter to do this either," Jelly Bean confessed. "But kids have dreams, and the more we resist, the more scathing tell-all books they'll write about us, right? I just don't want to be the subject in *Daddy Dearest!*"

Everyone laughed and Jelly Bean ducked back into his dressing room before I could ask him what he thought of my act. But of course he hadn't seen it. Still, it would have been nice to hear a few words of support and encouragement and maybe the promise of another gig.

But who knew if I'd ever see Jelly Bean again?

This could be my only chance.

"I'll meet you guys back in the room," I said to my family.

"Jelly Bean?" I said, meekly knocking on the open door when they had gone.

"Come in, Trixie."

Jelly Bean wiped his face with a handkerchief. The energy he gave to his audience left him exhausted after two shows — plus he drank, smoked, overate, and traveled continuously.

"I just want to thank you for making my life's dream come true," I began.

"And to think, I didn't even have to get naked," he said with a laugh.

"I hope you have a great show tomorrow. I mean, I know you will," I rambled. "I want to thank you for giving me the opportunity . . . Can I ask where you're going next?"

"Mexico. I'm shooting a movie. After that I'm taking time off to write my memoirs. I won't be back on the road till next year."

He reached for his scotch and got up.

"Do you have any suggestions for me?" I asked quickly.

"Keep studying—comedy and school," he said like a professional comic and a father. "But that's not what you want to hear, is it? This business is crazy, Trixie. Even for someone like me. You can have a blockbuster hit movie one year and be the national spokesperson for garbage bags the next. But as long as you have the drive, keep performing. You'll find your audience—and they'll find you."

"When I grow up, I want to be just like you!"

"Big and fat?"

"No," I laughed. "Making people laugh."

"You're already grown up, Trixie."

I hugged my idol with all my might before he turned to leave.

"I'd like to ask you something else," I said.

"You want my buffet ticket? Actually, I need two!"

"It's something I haven't had the nerve to ask you before—"

"Well, shoot. But my wife keeps the checkbook."

"Can I have your autograph?"

Sid wasn't at the roulette wheel, the blackjack table, the buffet, or the arcade. Knowing my brother, he was skipping the flash of Legends' neon for being flashed at a strip bar. Jelly Bean was plopped on a stool at the roulette wheel at Caesar's with his wife and a pound of doughnuts. My parents were fast asleep.

I was alone, wired, and starved. How could I have stomach pangs at a time like this? I scarfed down every soft drink and all the candy and snacks in the minibar while I flipped through the cable channels. I wished there was someone to share my shining moment with. I realized it was like celebrating a birthday by myself.

The red digital clock radio showed 3:45 A.M. Jazzy was with Ricky at some Chicago hotel after the prom. And what if Gavin had rented a room as well?

This had been the best night of my life. Yet as I sat on the edge of the bed with a Snickers bar and diet Coke watching *Bass Fishing with Bob* instead of reflecting on my Vegas debut, all I could think of was Gavin pinning a corsage on another girl.

BUSH GIRLS

M y first impulse when I arrived home was to call Gavin and tell him about my huge weekend. I pulled his senior year picture out of my drawer—where I'd hidden it after our fight—and replaced it on my dresser. I picked up the phone. Wouldn't he want me back now that I was home? Surely it would be okay to just say hi? But when I heard a ring I just as impulsively hung up. I put his picture back in the drawer and closed it tight.

But there was always Jazzy. I shared all my news with her at the Sunrise Coffee Shop. "Who cares about the prom when you're Vegas-famous! Douglas Douglas is going to scoop you up!" Jazzy shouted.

What if Douglas Douglas did call? What if I got my own TV show? Was I ready? I'd been waiting for this all my life! But I wanted Gavin to come with me. And the reality was that although yesterday I was in Vegas opening for Jelly Bean, tomorrow I'd be taking a social studies test.

After recounting every backstage moment to Jazzy, I had to get the prom buzz.

"Gavin showed up with some unknown airhead in a dress that screamed Kmart. My guess is her parents were first cousins! I can't tell you how long they stayed because Ricky got sick on the punch early. Or that's what I told my mom," she said, nudging me.

But I didn't laugh. Instead I envisioned Gavin as Prince Charming and his date as Cinderella.

"She had warts on her chin and a crooked nose," Jazzy said.

"Did he look happy?"

"How could he be happy without you?"

"Did I make the right choice?"

"You can't live in reverse. You're cruising in fifth gear now, and I'm not going to let anyone slow you down. The *Douglas Douglas Show* could call at any moment! You could be dating the talk show king himself. You'll totally forget a high school senior named . . . what was it again? Garret? Greg?"

"Thanks, but Douglas Douglas is fifty years old."

"And your point would be? Hello! He's a handsome fifty. I bet his beach house is quite gorgeous, and his bank account very attractive. You could be his sixth wife!"

All I could think of was what Gavin would look like at fifty. Certainly more handsome than Douglas Douglas.

★ ★ ★

"Trixie Shapiro?" a familiar voice called. I was lying on my lounge chair next to the sparkling pool at the Beverly Hotel, rubbing lotion into my fifty-year-old body, when a jet-black-haired man with the torso of a teenager eclipsed the sun.

"Gavin? I can't believe it's you!"

We hugged as if we were still lovers in high school.

"I read the People *article about you on the plane," he said. "You're doing everything you always wanted!"*

Just then a perky, blond, bikini-clad teenager slithered out of the water and waved to Gavin.

"Is that your daughter?" I asked.

"My daughter? No, she's my wife!"

My jaw dropped open.

"And you? I read you've split from Douglas Douglas."

"Yeah, he got tired of having to leave the studio when I performed. And I got tired of feeding him through a straw. Would you—"

"Gavin!" called the wife.

"Listen, I'd love to hear all about your life sometime, but. . . . It was great seeing you," he said. He gave me a quick good-bye kiss on the cheek before returning to his young bride.

I returned to my Beverly Hills hotel room and my fifteen cats.

★ ★ ★

My gig in Vegas was all over school. As Gavin's girlfriend, I'd received respectful glares from senior cheerleaders, but now I was getting solo invitations to hip parties and stares from freshman boys.

My first invite was for head cheerleader Jenny's baseball bash. This time I wasn't on the arm of Eddie or Gavin. I was center stage.

My head began to spin from the barrage of questions.

"What's Jelly Bean really like?" "Tell us a joke!" "Do you know Robin Williams?" It was a press conference. At least then I would have had an assistant fielding questions and writing my script. But onstage life hadn't prepared me for life offstage. Months ago I had been an anonymous girl who couldn't raise her hand in class to go to the bathroom. Now I fled to the bathroom to avoid attention.

Jazzy followed me there. "What are you doing?"

I splashed my face with cold water.

"Your fans await you," Jazzy exclaimed. "We're major populars now! Clark Fielding was hitting on me. Every guy wants you! Seth Martin wants to ask you out."

Seth Martin was a major hipster who had never even smiled at me.

"Can I open for Jelly Bean next time?" Jazzy joked. "I want everyone to love me!"

"They don't love me; they don't even know me."

"It doesn't matter. You are the IT Girl."

"Of course it matters. They aren't asking me anything about me—they're asking about Jelly Bean and Robin Williams. I don't even know Robin Williams."

"You're missing the point! We've always wanted to be popular. Now the whole school knows who you are, and they know me because I'm your best friend."

"This isn't what I thought being popular was," I confessed, leaning against the sink. "It's so superficial!"

"Duh! It's all about being superficial. Head cheerleader. Head jock. Now, head comedian. It's about time we knocked those athletes off their pedestals."

"I don't want to be superficial. I just want to belong. And I'm not sure being invited to hip parties makes me feel like I belong any more than when I sat at home weekends and watched videos."

"Trixie, we're not bush girls anymore."

"We'll always be bush girls. Just because I can walk onstage and tell a few jokes doesn't mean I'm not the same person inside."

"But you're not—you're much stronger. A year ago you couldn't even say hi to Gavin. Now you've said good-bye to him. You've come a long way, baby!"

"But I still love him, even more than I did that first day. I know he's not perfect, like I thought when I used to pass him in the hallway. And I love him even more for that."

"Well, fine, you can pout about your sudden celebrity, but I'm going to have fun. Clark Fielding asked me for my number!"

"What about Ricky?"

"He's not popular. But everyone wants to go out with Clark," she said, opening the door with a wicked grin. "See ya!"

I stepped out. Seth Martin was leaning against the wall in the dark hallway. "Heard you and Gavin are history," he said.

I didn't want Gavin and me to be "history." I wanted us to be a "current affair." But out of the corner of my eye I saw Gavin Baldwin leaning on the piano, stroking Jenny's hair. Not Jenny Larson! I thought he didn't want a ditzy bubblehead. I thought maybe now he'd be dating a sorority chick. But Jenny?

My heart ripped open and my lifeless body was filled with pain.

"I have to get some air," I said, pushing past Seth and stepping out onto the back porch.

"Can I get you a drink?" Seth called.

"Yes! Two—one for each hand!" I demanded, the screen door closing behind me. I staggered to the swing set.

A minute later I noticed Seth, again, standing in

front of me.

Seth was cute with his sparkling ice-blue eyes. He handed me the beer, and I watched him as he took a swig.

Then I stood up, grabbed him, pulled him to me, and kissed him long and hard, trying to kiss away Gavin from my mind.

We leaned against the frame of the swing set. Eventually Seth sat on the swing and pulled me onto his lap and we kissed again.

"So," he said, nuzzling in close. "Now you'll invite me to Vegas?"

I didn't speak much to Seth after that night. What had I been thinking?

I didn't tell anyone at school about the booker from the *Douglas Douglas Show*. I didn't want kids asking me every day if the show had called. But Sarge was another story.

"It's been two weeks!" she exclaimed, playing the saved phone messages while Dad watched ESPN and I stared at my History textbook. "I'm calling first thing in the morning!"

"You can't call! They don't talk to mothers."

"They need to be nudged," she argued, opening her mail.

"I thought you didn't want me to pursue comedy?"

"You may never get another chance like this again."

"I can't have my mother call the *Douglas Douglas Show!*"

"I'm not calling the show—I'm calling him!"

"That's crazy! You're not calling him! You're not! You could ruin any chances I have. Dad—," I whined. "She's not calling."

"I think your mother is right," my dad said, sitting up. "We've been talking about your career."

"My career?"

I probably should have been thrilled that my parents were sharing my ambition. Wasn't this what I wanted? Had I forgotten all those battles just to get their permission to perform at Chaplin's?

"Yeah, I'll be paid more at Chaplin's because I have a major credit now. I can't get more work from Jelly Bean because he's taking time off. I'll just have to wait."

"It seems a shame. You've got a hook. You're a teenage stand-up. That seems very marketable. It would be advantageous to get you noticed—"

"I thought you wanted me to go to school. Study. Be home early. Now you guys are talking about Douglas Douglas, hooks, and marketability?"

I felt a pressure to suddenly succeed. Wasn't I successful already?

"You're as good as any of those raunchy comics head-lining Chaplin's," Sarge declared.

"I just played Vegas—isn't that good enough?" I asked.

"All I'm saying is that Vegas is a good opportunity to get more exposure," my dad said.

"Stand-up used to be *my* dream. Now it's everyone's! Jazzy thinks I should have a star on Mason's front steps, the kids at school wonder when I'm going to be taping the sitcom *Shapiro,* and you two think I should be on *Oprah* promoting my memoirs."

I had struggled so hard to win Sarge's support, but now that she was supporting me, I wanted to hide in my bedroom. I wanted to fulfill my dreams, but without pressure or conflict—with Gavin by my side, and my parents' expectations complementing, not exceeding, my own.

I left my born-again stage parents and went into my bedroom to escape, the same way I'd always escaped, since I was a little girl. I lay back on my bed, stared at a hundred cutout faces of comedians, put my headphones on, and listened to Steve Martin's CD *Comedy Is Not Pretty!*

Laughter.

The very thing that had gotten me into this mess.

"Trixie, here's the yearbook!" Jazzy exclaimed, plopping the two-ton book in my lap as we sat on the bleachers during lunch the next day.

"Look, you were voted most likely! Look here, right by your picture!"

"Voted most likely to what?"

"Be a stand-up comedian!" Jazzy proclaimed proudly.

"Well, I already am, aren't I? That's no psychic prediction."

"Yeah, but they mean famous."

"And your senior picture is great! That's important, because when *Entertainment Tonight* finds this book years from now, it's best if you don't look like a total geek."

"What about you?" I asked, flipping through the pages.

"I was voted most likely to bleach my hair."

"No!"

"Well, duh! But here's a picture of us eating lunch together."

"That's so cool! You look fab." I continued leafing through the book. "Oh man!" I said, my heart sinking. "Here's one of me and Gavin by my locker."

Suddenly a freshman girl stood in front of me, staring. "Trixie, will you sign my yearbook?"

"Uh, sure," I said, startled.

"My name is Karen. Please write 'To Karen from your friend forever, Trixie Shapiro.'"

"But I don't even know you!"

"You're famous, get used to it," Jazzy whispered.

Three days later in study hall, Jazzy handed me a stack of yearbooks. "This is to Tracey Banks," she said, handing me a book. "I get three dollars for every signature. I'll give you half!"

"I can't sell my signature!"

"Then I won't give you half."

I must have signed every yearbook in Mason. Every yearbook—except one.

I was leaning against my locker when Gavin approached me.

"Will you sign mine?" he asked. He looked at me, a twinkle and a tear in his eye. I opened the book where the marker lay. It was filled with Chaplin's ticket stubs. Several spilled out onto the floor.

I looked back into his eyes, puzzled.

"I slipped into Chaplin's after you went onstage. I was always there," he confessed.

"Gavin," I said. "But why—"

"Shh," he said, closing the book and placing his finger over my lips. He leaned in and kissed me.

I spotted Gavin at the drinking fountain between classes, his red-vinyl yearbook tucked under his arm. I hung back, fiddling unnecessarily in my locker. When he glanced up, I offered him a smile. The bell rang and he hurried past me toward class. Frown number eleven. I slammed my locker and retreated into the crowd.

SEX, DRUGS, AND COMEDY

☆

A t Chaplin's Vic bumped me up to a feature act, and my paycheck more than doubled. Zach Price, fresh from his hit sitcom, was currently headlining. Jazzy was totally crushed out on him and begged to come to the club. I agreed, if she promised to arrive after my set.

"I can't believe we're going to party with Zach Price!" Jazzy said wildly as we knocked on his door at the Amber Hills Hotel after the show.

"Shhh! He'll hear you," I whispered.

Zach flung open the door. "Come on in, girls!" he said, drunk. The small room was filled with girls. I think every waitress from Chaplin's was there.

"Beer?" he asked.

"Sure!" Jazzy said.

"What do you mean 'sure'!" I whispered.

We squeezed through the crowd of partygoers in the tiny hotel room.

Zach was the life of the party. It was his job. Wherever there was an audience, Zach was the clown. He started telling anecdotes and acting out stories and doing perfect impressions of Douglas Douglas.

The life of the party was a real professional. Jazzy, the waitresses, and I giggled wildly at his stories. Zach shamelessly flirted with us, pulled Jazzy's skirt and grabbed my tush when I wasn't looking.

He lit a joint, took a hit, and held it out to Jazzy.

"Want some?"

"Sure!" Jazzy exclaimed.

"You don't—," I started.

"I do!" Jazzy screamed. She hopped onto the edge of the bed next to Zach. She took a long drag of the joint and held her breath. Then she went into a coughing frenzy as the smoke filled her virgin lungs.

They passed it back and forth while I sat on the floor, doodling on the hotel stationery for what seemed like an eternity.

"I'm hungry!" Jazzy said, lying back on the bed, her eyes heavy and red.

"Want some coke?" Zach asked.

"I'm hungry, not thirsty," Jazzy snapped.

"I'm not talking about drinking!" he said with a laugh.

"No thanks." I dragged Jazzy to the vending machine at the end of the hall. "With all the waitresses at

Chaplin's getting stoned in Price's room, I'm afraid it's going to be self-service."

"I want chips. A Snickers bar. Two Snickers bars," Jazzy said. "And pretzels."

I wound up spending five dollars on munchies.

"I don't feel any different," she whispered. "Really. I don't know what the big whoop is! I thought I'd see snakes."

But when she laughed, she couldn't stop.

I dragged her out of the hotel, but she resisted.

"Hey, his room's that way!"

"I'm taking you home—"

"But Zach boy's expecting us!"

"You're grounded," I said in my best Sarge impression.

As we walked to the parking lot, I wondered: If this is success, how do people handle failure? I didn't want to spend my life having to find an artificial rush while I was pursuing the real one.

Though Zach was a hilarious host, I felt like Jazzy and I had just attended a high school drugsters happening instead of an adult celebrity's party.

Would life on the road be the same for a girl? Would I have groupies like a rock star? Not likely. I'd probably only be hit on by the booker or the male comedians and prefer to sit alone in my hotel room, flipping channels like Cam had.

As I began to drive Jazzy home, I realized that though it was a challenge to be alone onstage, it might be a bigger challenge to be alone offstage.

THE *DOUGLAS DOUGLAS SHOW*

☆

I was staring out the window in Anatomy class when a secretary from the principal's office arrived to inform me I had a phone call.

It had to be an emergency. Had Sarge been sucked into the vacuum cleaner? Had Dad been caught between the couch cushions? Was Sid lying lifelessly in his war-torn dorm, an empty pack of cigarettes crumpled in his outstretched hand?

"Douglas Douglas!" Sarge screamed into the phone.

"Mom—are you okay? Calm down!"

"Douglas Douglas!" she screamed again.

"Is he dead? Don't tell me he's dead!"

"No! He's alive and you've been booked on his show!"

"That's your economy fare? For that price I could buy the plane," Sarge yelled into the phone to some hapless reservations clerk as I burst through the door.

My gig on the *Douglas Douglas Show* would net me five hundred dollars, two nights' accommodations at the Tropical Hotel, and two round-trip airline tickets. But Sarge wanted to go, so she had to buy another ticket.

"The airlines are robbing me blind," she said to me, covering the mouthpiece. "I used up all our frequent-flier miles for Vegas. I'd buy a ticket on the Internet, but those companies fold every other day!" Then she said into the phone, "Don't they give celebrity discounts? My daughter's a star!"

I grabbed a Coke from the fridge. I still couldn't believe I was going to be on TV!

"I have to be there," she said, covering the receiver again. "I have to help you with your makeup."

"Mom, they have people for that," I said.

"Yes, and they call them mothers."

"Super!" she said, suddenly pleased, into the phone. "Chicago . . . to Detroit . . . to Dallas . . . to San Francisco . . . to L.A.? I could walk faster!"

"Ma, you don't have to come," I said. "Dad will be there."

"That's as good as it gets?" she continued. "Well . . . all right then. I'd like two seats . . . one by the window. Oh. There isn't reserved seating? Is there toilet paper on this flight, or do I have to bring that too?"

I rolled my eyes. As if I wasn't nervous enough, now I'd have to worry about Sarge missing a connection.

"I should get there just in time for Douglas Douglas' retirement," she said with a smile.

After I nibbled on caviar and gossiped with Bette Midler in the greenroom of the Douglas Douglas Show, *an assistant escorted me to the stage. The famous red-velvet curtains pulled back to thunderous applause and a standing ovation. I smiled and walked to my mark. I turned to the camera and performed flawlessly. After taking my final bow, I was greeted by Douglas, who kissed me on the cheek and flirted with me for the rest of the segment. During commercial break, he leaned over and whispered, "I'd like to make a proposal."*

"Marriage? But I could be your granddaughter!"

"I'm proposing another kind of partnership. I'd like to produce the Trixie Shapiro Show!*"*

I tossed and turned all night in my king-sized bed at the Tropical Hotel. I couldn't even enjoy the pool the next day. I was in a coma, my eyes glazed over, terrified of what might happen when I arrived at the studio. Sarge hadn't arrived at the hotel and wasn't answering her cell phone. The limo had arrived to whisk us to the studio when the concierge raced over.

Sarge was fogged in at the Dallas airport. I came out of my coma with a sigh of delight.

Desperate farmers pray for rain—desperate comics pray for fog.

I may not have made the cheerleading squad or honor roll, but my name was one of the chosen few on the security guard's list at the gate to Pacific Studios.

Theme park magic filled me as I passed actors, technicians, trailers, VIP parking spaces, caterers with trays of cold cuts.

In the massive studio, more suited for a 747 than a few stand-up comediennes, I was met by a talent coordinator, a perky girl who had preinterviewed me on the phone.

She led me down the hallway into a dressing room—my dressing room!—where a gift basket awaited me. I should be giving *them* gifts.

A male assistant came in and asked if I needed anything pressed. Before I could answer, he whisked away my garment bag.

"I'll have this back in a jiffy!"

I fiddled with my gift basket until he returned. A Swatch watch, a bottle of CK One, a bag of Godiva chocolates, and a Sony Walkman. These were better gifts than I got for my sixteenth birthday.

I impatiently put on my black tights, black-vinyl skirt, paisley blouse, and ankle-high boots. I was called to makeup, where I was smothered by a huge smock so my clothes wouldn't be stained with powder. This was way cooler than when Jazzy and I attempted hairdressing. I felt like a movie star, being coiffed, sprayed, and powdered by a Hollywood professional.

Back in my dressing room I waited on pins and needles for the show to start. I wondered why there weren't food and drinks, although I was too nervous to eat and was already peeing my brains out without more diet Coke. I watched the TV monitors as the cohost warmed up the audience. I just hoped Dad wasn't sitting in the front row.

I went into the hallway to pace and bumped into a man.

"Excuse me," I apologized, looking up. It was every teenybopper's fantasy—pop star Creole!

"You're Creole!" I gasped. "My best friend has all your CDs!"

"And you don't?"

"Well . . . I have mostly comedy CDs."

"Yeah, I haven't made many of those. But if I don't get some tea, my song might turn out to be quite hilarious," he said, and disappeared into his own dressing room.

I had just told Creole I didn't have his CDs. Was I insane?

I returned to the safety of my dressing room. Douglas Douglas was beginning his monologue. I tried not to bite my nails, so I chewed on my knuckles instead. "We have a great show," he said. "Creole, Fred Buckley from the

Cincinnati Zoo, and teenage comedienne Trixie Shapiro!"

"Oh my God!" I screamed, as if I had just won at bingo.

The talent coordinator rushed in. "I heard a scream!"

"Uh . . . I thought I saw a mouse. But—"

The talent coordinator spoke into her walkie-talkie. "Jerry, did the zoo guy bring any rodents?"

The next thing I knew three guys were in my dressing room hunting for my imaginary Mickey.

I snuck out of the dressing room. "Agh!" I screamed again, suddenly face-to-face with an unimaginary white tiger!

"He won't bite," Fred Buckley said, holding the leash much too loosely for my comfort.

"Couldn't you have brought a goldfish? They don't bite either."

At this point I couldn't wait to go onstage. Not even in Algebra class had the minutes passed more slowly.

I returned to my dressing room and tried not to throw up.

I watched Creole sing his latest hit, "Electric Elegance." I envisioned Jazzy freaking out at home in Chicago.

I went to the bathroom.

Returned to find Creole making small talk with Douglas.

Re-applied lipstick. Cracked knuckles. Stretched out back.

Saw commercial break—made bathroom break.

Watched Fred Buckley feed possum. Checked makeup.

Watched Douglas Douglas feed possum. Stared at clock.

Wished possum had eaten in Cincinnati.

Another commercial break. Bit nails. Shook out hands. Checked clock.

Watched Fred Buckley go overtime—his white tiger kept licking Creole, whose manager was freaking out in the hallway. "If that tiger eats my client . . ."

Watched Fred's peacock escape and flutter around George Edwards and his Studio One Orchestra.

Checked clock. I was being upstaged by a bird!

Checked clock again—why hadn't I been called? Was this show filmed in two parts?

Zillionth commercial break.

Checked clock again. Prayed for sequel.

Animal assistant carried possum offstage.

Reality hit—the show was almost over, and I hadn't even performed!

My head was dizzy from staring at clock. Douglas went to yet another commercial. I paced the hallway. Had I missed my cue? Had the talent coordinator been abducted by aliens?

I was about to run to the potty yet again when she returned and, without explanation, rushed me to the closed studio door, above which flashed an intimidating red light. I could hear applause from the other side.

"You won't be able to perform," the talent coordinator quickly whispered.

"What do you mean?" I asked anxiously, my stomach sinking. All my lines were rehearsed. What would I say? What would I do?

"Unfortunately we've run out of time," I heard Douglas Douglas announce. "But let's at least bring her out—teenage comedienne Trixie Shapiro!"

Everyone was watching—Sarge, Dad, Sid, Jazzy, all of Mason High, and every relative my mom could use her long-distance dollars to call, and who knew who else? Jelly Bean. Steve Martin. The president. Maybe even my long-lost love, Gavin Baldwin, was tuned in.

Suddenly the grand red-velvet curtain opened from the wing of the stage. I saw the bright spotlights, the clapping audience, and a charming silver-haired Douglas Douglas standing behind his mahogany desk. My skin tingled. I felt dizzy from the sudden rush of attention.

I awkwardly walked out with a wide, cheesy, twitching smile. I had been instructed to go to the painted mark in the middle of the stage, but now that I wouldn't be performing, I wasn't sure where to go.

The legendary host shook my hand. Then Douglas Douglas waved me over to The Seat.

Every comedian's dream is to sit in The Seat.

"It's nice to meet you, Mr. Douglas," I whispered, trying not to shout. Like a thousand times before, he turned to the camera and said, "You can call me Douglas!"

I sat down in The Seat. The crowd laughed and applauded as Creole, the cohost, Douglas Douglas, and I then waved good-bye.

That was it. That was me in the big time. That was me on the *Douglas Douglas Show*.

Andy Warhol theorized that every person gets fifteen minutes of fame. If that was true—I was owed fourteen minutes and thirty seconds.

LA LA LAND

'd been searching for myself since the day I was born, and for all its terror and uncertainty, the stage was where I found myself. In the real world I was just a shrimp, ignored, overwhelmed, and dominated by my mother. But onstage I was in control; the stage was home.

When I reflected on how far I had traveled, I felt astonished, as if my childhood dreams had been ordinary and my experiences over the last few months the real dream. I'd made thousands of people laugh, schmoozed with TV stars, played Vegas, and appeared, however briefly, on the *Douglas Douglas Show.*

I certainly hadn't gotten this far on my own. Without Jazzy, Mr. Janson, Eddie, Cam, my dad, even Sarge, I'd still be plucking pricklies from my hair. But only I could choose which road to take now.

I had risen from class mime to class comedienne.

Now that I'd lived my dream, what should I dream of next?

★ ★ ★

"So are we going to share an apartment? Or should we join a snobby sorority?" Jazzy asked after announcing her acceptance from Northwestern. "We could be Alpha-Beta Rollerbladers!" She laughed as we sat at the Sunrise Coffee Shop, getting a quick fix before a day of exams.

I picked at my straw.

"Hey, we don't have to join a sorority," Jazzy said. "We can join a fraternity!"

I flicked a crumb off the table.

"You're not laughing, Trix. Do you want to live at home? That's okay—we can save money. But the second year we absolutely have to move out."

"I'm not going," I said.

"Not going to move out?"

"I'm not going to Northwestern."

"Oh. Did you apply somewhere else?" she asked, confused.

I shook my head.

"You mean you didn't apply? But you told me—"

"I didn't get accepted, Jazzy."

"That's unbelievable! You've just been on the *Douglas Douglas Show!*"

"Well, I wasn't really on it, now was I? Besides, they don't ask about things like that on the SAT."

"Maybe you can retake it. There must be a way to get

255

you in. Could Jelly Bean call?"

"Jazzy, I don't want to go to college now."

"Are you crazy?"

"I want to move to L.A."

"You *are* crazy!"

"Well, my uncle Redmond has a beachfront condo. I can sleep on his sofa until I can afford a place of my own."

"California? That's halfway across the world! We're supposed to stay together."

"I know," I said ambivalently. "But the business is out there. TV, agents, managers, tons of comedy clubs. The *Douglas Douglas Show.* I have to keep going while things are hot."

"Why didn't you tell me all this? I thought we'd be sorority sisters. Or share a swank apartment and have college hotties stopping over for late-night studies!"

"I really wanted to. . . ," I said, biting my straw.

"No you didn't. This is what you've always wanted."

I paused, then said, "That's why I have to give it a shot."

"But everyone is so plastic out there. You'll be miles away from me."

"You can visit me," I offered. "I'll be on the beach— Muscle Beach."

"You'll have to have a car," she rambled. "You can't

take a bus or train all the time like here."

"I know," I said, imagining myself driving around the freeway in a dump truck.

"And you're not going to college?" she asked, pulling at her scone.

"If I live in California for five years, I can get free in-state tuition."

"Five years? You'll be an old woman!"

I laughed. "Now you're being crazy." I took a long sip of my iced coffee as I pictured myself a fifty-year-old student.

"I can't believe we won't be hanging out every day," she said, staring out the window.

"Want to come with me?" I asked eagerly.

"Me in L.A.?" she asked, shocked. "That's Babesville USA! I'd have to get implants, tucks, and permanent eyebrows just to keep from looking forty. I can't afford it!"

The fear I was hiding inside me started to surface.

"You're right, Jazz," I said, suddenly pensive. "How do I think *I'm* going to get noticed? The babes out there make Stinkface look like a circus freak."

"Don't worry," she reassured me. "You have talent. You can't get surgery for that."

"There are a million people in L.A. with talent," I moaned.

"But you are really unique. And brave."

"Brave? I'm terrified," I said, my stomach knotting up. "I'll be leaving everything behind. How do I think I'm going to make it there? Sid is broke in Illinois and he shares rent with three other guys. I'm sure I'll be eating Ramen noodles for the rest of my life."

"Whatever!" she encouraged me. "You've rocked in Chicago and in Vegas. L.A. will love you."

"You and my parents will be days away from me. I'll be in another time zone. I'll be breaking up the bush girls."

"A dream can't separate us that easily! We'll have videophones and the Internet. And don't forget about beach vacations. I'll have to escape the arctic Chicago winter."

"When you visit, you can have Uncle Redmond's couch," I offered.

"You bring the surfer dudes and I'll bring the sunscreen," she said, excited.

We gathered our school gear and headed for the door. I stared at my best friend as she fixed her hair in the window's reflection.

"I'm going to be so lonely without you!" I said with a lump in my throat.

"You'll forget all about being lonely when you're onstage," she said, putting her arm around me. "And when you're not onstage, you call me."

★ ★ ★

Early that summer Sarge bawled her eyes out when she and Dad left Uncle Redmond's Venice beach condo, after helping me settle in.

"You take care of her," she called to her younger brother as the taxi waited. "Or I'll pull your ears like I did when you were little!"

"And she did," he whispered to me. "One ear's longer than the other."

I laughed, but it only eased the pang of separation for a moment, the same pang I had felt when dropped off at sleepover summer camp in the third grade. But I knew this stay would be longer than two months, and I'd have to take care of my own meals.

Uncle Redmond was almost louder than Sarge, a boisterous man, always screaming real estate deals into the phone. But he wasn't a chore master like his sister. In fact I found myself cleaning up after him. I had to come to Hollywood to learn how to be a housewife.

But it was worth it just to be near the ocean. I had never seen a more breathtaking sight than the view from his living-room window. Surfers and sunsets, plus a boardwalk crowded with hippie vendors, fortune-tellers and palm readers, a seventy-year-old lady dancing in a bikini, and countless runners, walkers, skateboarders, and Rollerbladers.

For the next six months I worked at Tootsie's Diner to

help with expenses. Uncle Red said, "This could help your career," as if a movie director is dying to find the "right waitress." The restaurant business was as raunchy as stand-up. I even got heckled when I brought the check. In the meantime I waited for prospective managers and agents to return my phone calls. I called the *Douglas Douglas Show* show every week, and every week I hung up, intimidated by the receptionist.

I began to feel homesick. I wondered where I really belonged.

I couldn't make a girl friend to save my life. There was no one like Jazzy. Every girl I met was always looking past me to see what producer or director was walking by, as if she was the newest IT Girl. I met several career surfers who must have taken one too many spills and several forty-year-old men Uncle Red knew who had never been married.

"Maybe there's a reason," I whispered to him at dinner.

The ironic thing was that in L.A. there was no Chaplin's around the corner to do a quick set. There were certainly more clubs, but every comic in the world was dying to audition for the star maker, agent, or manager who might be sitting in the audience. I had to sign up months in advance just to get an open mike. Or camp out in a line for hours just to get a spot at one thirty in the morning.

I missed my family and Jazzy. I even missed the rain. I missed the one thing I had moved out here to do—perform. I needed that rush, that high, that peace.

After I dropped an order of chili fries on myself at Tootsie's, I slipped over to the pay phone and called Cam.

"I need your help," I said. "I'm stuck—"

"You've got a flat? You'll have to call Triple A, babe. I'm in Denver."

"I mean I'm stuck careerwise. I need a gig! It's been ages since I've performed, and I'm wondering why I'm out here."

"Trixie, your orders are piling up in the window!" the diner manager barked.

"Sounds like your career is calling you," he teased.

"If I'm forty years old and am still wearing an apron to work, please shoot me."

"Don't give up. You'll just have to go on the road, babe. I could get you some college gigs. But you'll have to live out of a suitcase. I don't know if that's the best place for a young girl like you."

"It can't be worse than living on a couch or slinging food all day for tourists who keep saying, 'Hey, waitress, you're so funny! You should perform stand-up.' And then they hide the tip in the ketchup bottle."

"Sounds like you need a vacation. But this isn't going to be the Bahamas. This is going to be Dayton, Ohio."

"Thanks, Cam. I love ya!"

"We'll see if you still feel that way after you've played Dayton."

STANDING ROOM ONLY

One year later, I was back in Chicago. I had a gig. At Chaplin's. Headlining. Not only had I changed, but Chaplin's had too. The brick wall behind the stage now had a neon bowler hat and cane to accompany the Chaplin's sign. There was new carpeting and Vic had converted his office into a dressing room. There was even extra toilet paper in the bathrooms.

I looked around the crowd, squinting to see my friends and family in the back row. Most people reserve the front row—Trixie Shapiro reserves the back.

I saw my parents, Sid, Jazzy with a new beau, Mr. Janson, Aunt Sylvia, Eddie, and Ben. Now that I knew where they were, I wouldn't look back there until I had finished my set. A flood of memories from the last year on the road rushed through me as I sat in the comforting surroundings of home.

But as I continued to scan the crowd, another familiar face appeared. There he was, sitting with an elderly

263

couple, as dreamy as the first time I had seen him in Mason's parking lot.

What if I forgot my new material? What if my timing was off? What if a table heckled me, and threw off my whole entire set?

But I was a professional now—I had been heckled, I had bombed, and though I'd come offstage many a night with scratches and wounds, I'd survived the thorny shrubberies of the road without Jazzy to rescue me.

True to his word, Cam had given my name to bookers around the country. I featured, headlined, and played fund-raisers and festivals. I e-mailed and phoned Jazzy and Sarge from every hotel in the country.

I loved college gigs the most, because they paid well and the audiences were young, educated, and hip. Yet watching couples holding hands made me feel disconnected, and reminded me of the sacrifice I was making.

I'd made new friends along the journey and gained confidence, experience, and a thick skin. My standard act was as much a part of me as my orange hair.

"It's great to be back at Chaplin's, where I got my start. I'm living alone in L.A. now. . . . Man, dating sucks!" I said, taking a beat. "If they can send a man to the moon . . . why can't they send one to my apartment?"

The crowd laughed. I felt the familiar jolt of exhilaration. The crowd took on a personality of its own. I rolled through my set with the confidence of the professional that I had become.

I left the stage feeling I could conquer the world.

"It was good seeing you again!" Ben said, catching up to me in the dressing room.

"It's great having you back," Vic said with a hug. "You're not a mousy girl anymore. You're a woman!"

"And you're a married man—," I reminded him with feigned shock.

"You better get out there," Vic said. "Your fans await you."

Sergeant rushed me like a linebacker and hugged me hard, while Dad handed me flowers with a big squeeze and a kiss on the cheek.

"You need to eat more!" Sarge commanded. "You're skinnier than these roses."

"This is Greg," a freshly tanned Jazzy said, introducing me to her studly beau. "Greg, this is my best friend in the whole wide world."

Sid was next, stinking of beer and cigarettes. I was ready for him to call me "shrimp." Instead, he said, "My Stand-up Sister!"

Mr. Janson gave me a warm embrace. "I discovered her!" he said proudly.

"No, I did," Eddie countered. He looked exactly the same, except for his hat, which read MICHIGAN STATE instead of PIZZA TOWN.

Jazzy pulled my arm and pointed to a lone hunkster hidden in the shadows, leaning against a pillar.

"He's alone!" she whispered, nudging me. "No Stinkface, no Jenny Larson!"

Everyone filed out, leaving Gavin and me alone to talk, something we hadn't done in over a year. Our last words had been good-bye.

Gavin looked as good as ever, wearing a black-and-white bowling shirt, blue jeans, and a black woolen jacket. His jet-black hair had grown longer, and a smooth goatee sprouted beneath his luscious mouth. For all my experience with improvisation, I couldn't think of anything to say. I was no longer the headliner at Chaplin's, but a bush girl again, awkward and shy.

"Congratulations," Gavin said, approaching me slowly, standing close, but stopping short of hugging me. "Your show was . . . wonderful."

"Thanks," I said, wanting to smother him with kisses. But I kept my arms at my sides. "I'm surprised you came. I saw you from onstage," I admitted.

"So I guess I don't make you nervous anymore?"

"Well, I didn't go blank," I answered. "But you still make me nervous!" I paused. "Jazzy's waiting," I finally said, not moving. "It was great seeing you again."

"I wanted to thank you," he said awkwardly.

"Thank *me*?"

"For being brave enough to follow your dream."

"But I thought you resented it."

"I did. But you also inspired me to start dreaming."

"You're not going to be an architect?" I asked, confused.

"Of course I am. But I realized it is okay to have a hobby."

I thought back on our conversation at his house about our dreams.

"You're writing?"

"I'm taking some classes. I never would have allowed myself to, if it wasn't for you."

I stared at him in shock, my heart pounding.

"That's not all I've been dreaming about," he confessed, looking me in the eyes.

"Yes?" I asked curiously.

"Dating sucks, just like you say in your act. You don't have to be stuck in a hotel room in Spokane to be lonely. You can be on a college campus with a million girls and spend all your nights dreaming of the one that got away."

I was dumbfounded. Gavin had been dreaming of me?

"And Northwestern doesn't even offer room service!" I said, trying to ease my nerves.

He laughed, flashing that familiar sparkling smile.

I felt what I always felt was true—that things weren't finished. That we could talk forever, that we were still connected. But were we?

"All finished, Trixie?" Ben asked, flipping the stage lights out.

"I'm glad you came. Really," I said to Gavin awkwardly. "It was nice to see you again."

"Trixie," Gavin said, grabbing my arm.

"Yes?" I asked.

"I wanted to tell you something else," he began anxiously. "I want that day when we had a picnic in the park back."

"The picnic?"

"I just want that day at the picnic back. 'Cause I would have reacted differently," he said, looking into my eyes. "I wouldn't have made you choose."

I couldn't believe what I was hearing. Tears welled up in my surprised eyes.

"I counted your smiles in school," I confessed. "Since I first saw you in Mason's parking lot. I was up to smile number nine when we started dating—and then it happened so often, I lost track! After the picnic you never smiled at me again, and I haven't been the same. . . . But since you smiled at me tonight, I guess I can start counting again. You're on number three."

"How about the part where you lose track," he said, hinting.

Once again, feeling like I'd won the lottery, not believing it was happening, I was lost in his hipster spell.

"I'd like to get to know you again."

"But you know that I travel. . . ," I began.

"I could build you a mobile home, with a white picket fence around it."

I was stunned. It was the sweetest thing I'd ever heard. "Don't joke with me, Gavin!"

"I'm serious—I'll leave the joking to you."

"I thought I'd never see you again. When I saw you tonight in the audience, I thought I'd freak out. But I think I even performed better knowing you were there."

He smiled a sparking smile.

"Number four," I said, pointing.

Ben placed my backpack and bottled water on the table next to me. "We're closing up, Trix," he said.

"I know! I know!" I said reluctantly, grabbing my sack. "I have to go—," I said, and opened the door to the lobby. "I'd like to read some of your writing . . . if you'd let me."

"Well, it took years before I could see you perform."

"I deserved that," I said with a cunning smile. "I'll be looking for it in the mail, then?" I asked, stepping back.

"How about I show it to you now. After you celebrate with your fans."

"I'd love to," I said with a smile. "So you're writing poetry?"

"I started writing a novel," he confessed. "I may never finish it, but . . . it's called *Comedy Girl*."

My heart melted.

"*Comedy Girl?*" I repeated, shocked, and put my hand to my mouth.

"Hey, don't cover those lips," he said, pulling my hand away. But instead of letting go, he held on.

Our fingers entwined. My heart raced.

He stared into my eyes just as he had done on our first date. And then he leaned over and kissed me.

Our arms wrapped around each other and I squeezed his body close to mine, as if I would never let go. I thought I was going to explode.

He kissed me again and grabbed my hand, opening the door for me.

"You can hang at my place anytime," he offered. "It's not a hotel room, but it's the same size," he joked. "I can break a bar of soap in half to make you feel at home."

"Your own apartment?" I exclaimed. "Maybe college isn't so bad! Do they have room for a class mime?"

Everything looked a little smaller at 1414 Chandler Street. The couch that used to swallow me was in fact only a love seat. The enormous kitchen table that I had to clean was barely large enough for a medium pizza.

I opened the door to my lavender room, which was now powder blue. The posters of my comic idols, some of whom I'd since met, were no longer taped to the walls, and there was an ugly patchwork quilt covering my bed. But Paddington Bear, Snoopy, Hello Kitty, and my other wide-eyed fluffy animals—my perfect audience—still sat loyally on my shelf where I had left them.

I opened my closet and tried on the pale blue Groovy Garments dress that I had worn on my first date with Gavin. My old dresser, once cluttered with cosmetics, barrettes, and snapshots, seemed tiny.

I reached under my bed, looking for my most special treasure. Was it gone, I thought as my fingers stretched wildly. Suddenly I felt the edge of a box—my comedy treasure chest full of notebooks, journals, a tape-recorded laugh track, and a round brush. And then I discovered lying in the bottom of the box the most important possession . . . my original comedy notebook. It sparkled even though it was worn. I hugged it as if I was hugging an old friend.

I stepped in front of my mirror, the mirror which no longer reflected a young girl but a young woman.

Instead of my usual Hollywood daydreaming, I reminisced.

A mother who brought me chicken soup in bed when I had the flu and took my temperature ten times a day. A devoted father who chaperoned me to Chaplin's. A brother who shared his innocent childhood moments with me, clowning around with a red nose and funny wigs. My first companions—scratched comedy CDs that skipped over punch lines when I played them. Endless days giggling through lunches with my priceless true-blue friend Jazzy, twigs poking through her radiant bleached-blond hair one year, and green barrettes the next. Trading blue nail polish for green, swooning over a cardboard cutout Leonardo, perusing through glam mags together in study hall. Receiving a million notes written in purple marker, talking for hours on the phone. Laughing until our stomachs threatened to explode. The smell of pizza on my clothes after an evening spent riding in Eddie's truck. The coolest man alive—Gavin Baldwin—smiling at me in the hallway, waiting for me at the Veins concert.

I opened my comedy notebook and, with my round brush as a microphone, read to the mirror, "I loathe high school. I'm unbearably shy, afraid to speak up in class. I'm not the class clown—I'm the class mime!" I snickered as a smile overcame my face.

All my life I'd been searching for myself in fantasy worlds, but now I was beginning to find myself in the real world. And the journey had only begun. Me. Trixie Shapiro. Comedy Girl.

ACKNOWLEDGMENTS

Special thanks to my dad, Gary, my armchair comedy coach, for knowing what is funny and, more importantly, what's not. My mom, Suzanne, for insisting I go into stand-up comedy and for always laughing the loudest. My brother Mark, for your wit and for paving the way for me to follow my dreams. And my brother Ben, the real stand-up comedian in the family.

Thanks to Katherine Tegen, a wonderful friend and editor, with a great sense of humor. Julie Hittman for your hard work and upbeat personality. And the friendly staff at HarperCollins.

ABOUT THE AUTHOR

A comedy girl herself, Ellen Schreiber was an actress and stand-up comedienne before becoming a full-time writer. She is the author of the novels TEENAGE MERMAID and VAMPIRE KISSES.

You can visit Ellen at her website:

www.ellenschreiber.com